A Trip to the Country

SERIES IN FAIRY-TALE STUDIES

General Editor
Donald Haase, Wayne State University

Advisory Editors
Cristina Bacchilega, University of Hawai'i, Mānoa
Stephen Benson, University of East Anglia
Nancy L. Canepa, Dartmouth College
Isabel Cardigos, University of Algarve
Anne E. Duggan, Wayne State University
Janet Langlois, Wayne State University
Ulrich Marzolph, University of Göttingen
Carolina Fernández Rodríguez, University of Oviedo
John Stephens, Macquarie University
Maria Tatar, Harvard University
Holly Tucker, Vanderbilt University
Jack Zipes, University of Minnesota

*A complete listing of the books in this series
can be found online at wsupress.wayne.edu*

A Trip to the Country

by Henriette-Julie de Castelnau, Comtesse de Murat

EDITED AND TRANSLATED BY

PERRY GETHNER AND ALLISON STEDMAN

Introduction by Allison Stedman

Wayne State University Press   Detroit

15 14 13 12 11   5 4 3 2 1

LIBRARY OF CONGRESS CATALOGING-IN-PUBLICATION DATA

MURAT, HENRIETTE JULIE DE CASTELNAU, COMTESSE DE, 1670–1716.
[VOYAGE DE CAMPAGNE. ENGLISH]
A TRIP TO THE COUNTRY / BY HENRIETTE-JULIE DE CASTELNAU, COMTESSE DE MURAT ;
EDITED AND TRANSLATED BY PERRY GETHNER AND ALLISON STEDMAN ;
INTRODUCTION BY ALLISON STEDMAN.
P. CM. — (SERIES IN FAIRY-TALE STUDIES)
INCLUDES BIBLIOGRAPHICAL REFERENCES AND INDEX.
ISBN 978-0-8143-3503-1 (PBK. : ALK. PAPER)
1. COUNTRY LIFE—FRANCE—FICTION. I. GETHNER, PERRY. II. STEDMAN, ALLISON, 1974–
III. TITLE.
PQ1875.M8V6913 2011
843'.4—DC22
2010048022

PUBLISHED WITH THE ASSISTANCE OF A FUND ESTABLISHED BY THELMA GRAY JAMES
OF WAYNE STATE UNIVERSITY FOR THE PUBLICATION OF FOLKLORE AND ENGLISH STUDIES.

DESIGNED AND TYPESET BY MAYA RHODES
COMPOSED IN ADOBE GARAMOND

Contents

Acknowledgments

Funding for the research and preparation of this manuscript was provided by a Bucknell University International Travel Grant (2005); a Bucknell University Center for the Study of Race, Ethnicity and Gender Summer Research Grant (2006); and a University of North Carolina at Charlotte Faculty Research Grant (2008). Many thanks to Alison Slater and John Westbrook, who provided assistance with an early draft of the first twenty pages of the manuscript; to Perry Gethner, whose expertise and hard work made the project viable; to my father David Stedman, who proofread the first completed draft; and to the students of "French 325: Literature and the Enlightenment" at Bucknell University (Spring Semester 2005), whose enthusiasm for the novel made me realize that the project was worth doing in the first place. My husband David M. Fillmore Jr., my mother Peggy Stedman, and my mother-in-law Sheila Fillmore provided crucial moral and logistical support; my involvement in this project would not have been possible without them. Nicholas Price, of Nicholas Price Fine Art (55 Cathles Road, London SW12 9LE), generously provided a copy of the book cover engraving, free of charge. We would also like to thank Faith E. Beasley, Henriette Goldwyn, Donald Haase, and Gabrielle Verdier for believing in the project and for their unfailing support and encouragement.

ALLISON STEDMAN

Introduction

{ALLISON STEDMAN}

Henriette-Julie de Castelnau, Countess de Murat, was born in Paris in 1668 into a prominent military family with long-standing ties to the sword nobility.[1] Both of her grandfathers, Jacques de Mauvissière, Marquis de Castelnau, and Louis Foucault, Count de Daugnon, had been marshals of France during Louis XIV's minority,[2] and her father, a colonel during the Franco-Dutch War (1672–78), died near Utrecht during the siege of Ameyden when Henriette-Julie was still a young child. Although her father was governor of Brest at the time of her birth and her mother, Louise-Marie Foucault de Daugnon, had family ties to the Limousin region, contemporary epistolary correspondences indicate that

1. Although nineteenth-century literary biographies such as Michaud's *Biographie universelle* and L. P.'s *Répertoire universel des femmes célèbres* maintain that Murat was born in Brest in 1670, more recent studies dispute this claim. Édouard Guitton's "Madame de Murat ou la fausse ingénue," Sylvie Cromer's introduction to Murat's *Edition du Journal pour Mademoiselle de Menou*, and the 1996 *Le XVIIe siècle dictionnaire des lettres françaises*, collectively establish that Murat was in fact born in Paris in 1668. Cromer establishes the precise date of October 14, 1668, based on the manuscript genealogies of La Buzardière, a château in the province of Maine, where Murat retired at the end of her life. See Geneviève Patard's critical introduction to *Madame de Murat: Contes* for all sides of the debate over Murat's birth date, place of birth, marriage, and subsequent exile (Patard, *Madame de Murat*, 9–11).

2. During the Old Regime, the marshals of France were the royal court's most important officers of state. The Court of Marshals, a select group of noblemen appointed by the king, had as its primary peacetime function the prevention of duels through mediation and forcing would-be combatants to reconcile.

Henriette-Julie most likely spent the majority of her childhood in Paris,[3] where she would have received a worldly education typical of the Parisian aristocratic elite.[4]

In 1691 Henriette-Julie married the widowed military colonel Nicolas de Murat, Count de Gilbertez,[5] and quickly became a fixture of the Parisian literary scene just as the late seventeenth-century vogue of literary fairy-tale production was unfolding. At the salon of the Marquise de Lambert that Murat frequented starting in 1692, she socialized with two of the genre's earliest pioneers: the Countess d'Aulnoy, who had published the first literary fairy tale of the French tradition as an interpolated story in her 1690 *Histoire d'Hypolite, comte de Duglas* (Hypolitus, Earl of Douglas) and would go on to publish a total of twenty-five fairy tales by the end of the decade, and Catherine Bernard, whose 1696 novel *Inès de Cardoue, nouvelle espagnole* (Inès of Cordoba, a Novella Set in Spain) contained two more fairy tales as interpolated narratives.[6] In addition to frequenting Lambert's weekly gatherings, Murat also kept the company of her cousins Charlotte-Rose Caumont de la Force and Louise de Bossigny,

---

3. As Geneviève Patard points out, Murat and her family are mentioned frequently in the Marquise de Sévigné's letters throughout the 1670s, especially those dated January 5, 1674; May 31, 1675; August 12, 1675; July 3, 1676; and October 15, 1677. These letters detail the daily activities of the Parisian elite (Patard, *Madame de Murat*, 10). See also note 29 in the translation.

4. Nineteenth-century biographical sources give a different version of her formative years, claiming that the future author was raised in Brittany and that she made her first appearance at the royal court of Versailles at the age of sixteen dressed in the traditional peasant attire of the Breton region, to the delight of Queen Marie-Thérèse. No documentation from the period exists to support this account, however. As Auguste-Pierre Ségalen points out, by the time Murat turned sixteen, Queen Marie-Thérèse would have been dead for three years (Ségalen, "Madame de Murat et le Limousin," 77–94). For examples of what is now referred to as "the Breton legend," see Michaud's *Biographie universelle* and Miorcec de Kerdanet, *Notices chronologiques*, 205–6.

5. According to Ségalen, the Count de Murat had previously been married to Murat's cousin Marie de La Tour, who died two years later in 1688 (Ségalen, "Madame de Murat et le Limousin," 78; cited by Patard, *Madame de Murat*, 11). Nineteenth-century biographers claim that Murat had no children and that the "great Murat family" came to an end with the death of her husband. Sylvie Cromer, however, has found evidence that Murat had two sons (Patard, *Madame de Murat*, 11).

6. Marchal, *Madame de Lambert et son milieu*, 226.

Countess d'Auneuil, both of whom would go on to author major works of fairy-tale fiction. Toward the end of her life Murat would remember with fondness the animated ambiance of d'Aulnoy's own salon on the Rue Saint-Benoît,[7] and it was perhaps through d'Aulnoy that Murat became acquainted with Marie-Jeanne Lhéritier de Villandon, whose own literary fairy tales would appear in 1695 and 1705, interpolated into her collection of *Oeuvres meslées* (Mixed Works) and her novel *La Tour ténébreuse et les jours lumineux* (The Shadowy Tower and the Radiant Days). During her time in Paris, Murat also cultivated an enduring friendship and literary alliance with bourgeois author Catherine Bédacier, who published under her maiden name, Durand, and who interpolated fairy tales into both her 1699 novel *La comtesse de Mortane* (The Countess de Mortane) and her 1702 novel *Les Petits Soupers de l'été, de l'année 1699* (The Light Suppers of the Summer of the Year 1699).

Murat began her literary career in earnest during the mid-1690s. She submitted numerous poems to academic competitions and finally published *Mémoires de Madame la comtesse de M**** (Memoirs of the Countess de M***) in 1697, a two-volume collection of pseudomemoirs designed to serve as a response to Saint-Évremond's *Mémoires de la vie du comte D*** avant sa retraite* (Memoirs of the Life of Count D*** before his Retirement) that had appeared the previous year and portrayed women as fickle and incapable of virtue. Stating that the goal of her memoirs was to rehabilitate the reputation of women by showing that "appearances often deceive" and that misfortune rather than corruption is the primary reason for improper female behavior, Murat's *Mémoires* was an instant success and was republished three times over the course of the next two years in Lyons, Amsterdam, and London and even translated into English. This work would establish Murat not only as a respected novelist but also as a social theorist with a unique perspective on the responsibility of women to protect and defend one another. Rather than attributing women's poor reputation to the cruelty of men, the *Mémoires* blame instead "a pitiful lack of solidarity" among women; women are held accountable for initiating the majority of rumors about other women and are revealed as the first to believe and to perpetuate such division among their own ranks.[8]

7. Murat, *Journal pour Mlle de Menou*, 173–74.
8. Murat, *Mémoires de Madame la comtesse de M****, 2:395–96.

Murat would reprise the importance of female solidarity in almost all of her subsequent literary production. In *A Trip to the Country*, for example, the female narrator's refusal to allow the Count de Selincourt's inconstancy to interfere in her friendship with Madame d'Arcire exemplifies the ideal of female comportment that Murat had advanced in this earlier work.

At the insistence of Lhéritier, who had dedicated her fairy tale "L'adroite princesse" (The Clever Princess) to Murat in 1695,[9] Murat published three volumes of fairy tales between 1698 and 1699: the *Contes de fées* (Fairy Tales; 1698), the *Nouveaux contes des fées* (New Fairy Tales; 1698) and the *Histoires sublimes et allégoriques* (Sublime and Allegorical Stories; 1699). By the author's own admission, these fairy-tale collections were designed to serve as retaliation for the 1695–97 publication of Charles Perrault's *Histoires ou contes du temps passé* (Stories or Tales of Times Past), also known as the *Contes de ma mère l'oye* (Mother Goose Tales). The preface to Perrault's collection, which portrayed the fairy tale as an oral pedagogical genre intended for children and originating from the folk tales of peasants and wet nurses, had recently been reprised by such literary critics as the Abbé de Villiers in his *Entretiens sur les contes de fées* (Inquiries on Fairy Tales), first printed in December of 1698. Villiers's critique had exalted the didactic and generic succinctness of Perrault's collection of fairy tales and used the moral superiority of Perrault's alternative incarnation of the genre as his basis for decrying the lengthy, digressive, and descriptive salon fairy tales popularized by Murat and by the members of her literary circle. In the prefatory dedication to her final collection of fairy tales, Murat launched an explicit defense of the salon ideal of fairy-tale production and of the experimental hybrid novels into which such works were often interpolated, works that Villiers had criticized for moral impropriety and insipidity. While conceding that the plots of "mother goose tales" may indeed be derived from the "low and infantile occupations of servants and wet nurses," as Perrault claims, Murat takes pains to situate her own modern fairy tales and those of her contemporaries as the outcome of an alternative literary trajectory. Inspired by the Renaissance Italian novellas of Straparola, salon fairy tales

9. Lhéritier, *Oeuvres meslées*, 229–33.

are authored by "modern fairies" of great intelligence and eloquence and are intended to engage in sophisticated ways with the ideological climate of the early Enlightenment.[10] The popularity of her fairy-tale collections helped to gain Murat induction into the Accademia dei Riccovrati (Riccovrati Academy) of Padua on February 19, 1699, while excerpts from a volume of poetry, now lost, earned her one of the Academy of Toulouse's coveted *Jeux floraux* (Floral Games) prizes.[11]

Having achieved the official markers of international success, Murat became the first of her salon contemporaries to consider the future of the literary fairy tale in a society increasingly beholden to Cartesian reason. The *Voyage de campagne* (A Trip to the Country; 1699), which appeared only a few months after her third collection of fairy tales, represents the first of a series of attempts on the part of the author to shift the focus of the supernatural away from faraway kingdoms and into present-day France, transforming its literary manifestation of choice from the *conte de fées* ("fairy tale") to the *conte de revenants* ("ghost story"), a genre whose incarnation of the supernatural, in being grounded in the natural world, was more compatible with rational Enlightenment-style philosophical inquiry. In so doing Murat revives, for the purposes of discussion and entertainment, a genre that had appeared sporadically in experimental novelistic production of the 1660s and 1670s[12] and regularly in the popular contemporary literary review the *Mercure Galant* during the decade that followed, peaking in popularity between 1678 and 1682. During the 1690s, however, the ghost story's popularity among the worldly community had been largely eclipsed by the *Mercure Galant's* extended series on the ability of Cartesian reason to prove the immortality of the soul and to disprove the immortality of the body. This debate, which began in 1690 with the publication of an article titled "La Vanité des songes" (The Vanity of the Imagination) and continued sporadically through April 1698, appears to have removed the subject of ghosts from literary fiction and situated it instead squarely within the realm of high philosophy, where

10. Murat, *Histoires sublimes et allégoriques,* i–vi.

11. Ségalen, "Madame de Murat et le Limousin," 87; Murat, *Le Journal pour Mademoiselle de Menou,* 46–47.

12. Murat alludes directly to one such novel in the tale that the narrator uses to humiliate her rival Madame de Talemonte. See note 79 in the translation, p. 91.

the indisputability of absolute truths overshadows the individual's ability to relativize reason with truths taken from personal experience or from the experiences of others.[13] In restoring the ghost story to the realm of worldly debate in the context of her novel, Murat thus ultimately articulates the first implicit refusal of Cartesian rationalism as an absolute system, foregrounding instead the individual's prerogative to arrive at opinions independently and to entertain a variety of competing points of view. Murat's deep-seated belief that absolute rational systems should be tempered by individual experience provides a recurring theme throughout *A Trip to the Country*. While characters who are easily seduced by absolute rational systems are mocked (as in the case of Selincourt's provincial neighbors), those who refuse to allow philosophy to replace the individual's ability to reason on his or her own terms are exalted (as in the case of the Duke's former love interest, Madame de Rantal).

In popularizing the ghost story as the novel's most prevalent interpolated genre, Murat simultaneously allows the spirit of rational Enlightenment debate to call into question a variety of concepts and distinctions taken as absolutes under the Old Regime social system. Not only is the nature and existence of ghosts left open to the reader to decide, but the essence of the noble identity is continually called into question in the context of the interpolated ghost stories. Is there indeed something innate about the noble identity of aristocrats, as the supernatural validation of the interpolated ghost story of La Motte Thibergeau would seem to suggest? Or is it time for aristocrats to take a more proactive bourgeois approach to self-definition, submitting their identities to rational deliberation just as the paranormal is submitted to such scrutiny in the story of Madame Deshoulières?

In *A Trip to the Country*, not only does the ghost story replace the fairy

---

13. Two notable exceptions to this are the anonymous satires of Louis XIV's newfound piety owing in part to the influence of his morganatic wife Madame de Maintenon, whom he secretly married in 1683. While in *Scarron apparu à Madame de Maintenon* (Scarron's Appearance to Madame de Maintenon; 1694), the king's wife is rebuked by the ghost of her former husband, in *L'esprit familier du Trianon, ou l'apparition de la duchesse de Fontange* (The Familiar Spirit of the Trianon, or the Apparition of the Duchess de Fontange; 1695) both Louis XIV and Madame de Maintenon are confronted by the king's former mistress.

tale as the most popular interpolated genre but also the only fairy tale included in the novel is modified to achieve its happy ending through a series of plot developments that both eliminates the need for fairy intervention and undermines the intrinsic relationship between nobility and social elitism. The novel's interpolated fairy tale, often referred to as "Le Père et ses quatre fils" (The Father and His Four Sons), is unique to late seventeenth-century literary production in its explicit omission of fairies, whom the narrator professes to exclude to see whether or not she can find a way to help the characters improve their fates without the aid of "these good women." The aristocratic narrator's challenge to herself is echoed on the level of plot when the tale's central character, the father, defies the long-standing cognatic system of aristocratic inheritance by splitting his fortune equally among his four aristocratic sons and sending them abroad to augment their fortunes by learning trades, a decision that ultimately serves to orchestrate the family's upward social mobility when the trades they learn prove useful to the king. As fairy magic in tales of this period generally serves to affirm the innate nature of the noble identity,[14] the tale's replacement of enchantment with excellence in a particular trade ultimately calls into question the degree to which the notion of nobility as an absolute barometer of social distinction can continue to function in the emerging Age of Enlightenment if nobles are unable to rise to the challenge of social self-determination.

Murat's desire to test the limits of social conventionality was not only apparent in her literary production, however. As is attested by the Count de Pontchartrain's administrative correspondence and the reports of Parisian lieutenant general of police René d'Argenson, such unconventionality was also apparent in Murat's personal life. On December 6, 1699, just after *A Trip to the Country* first appeared in print, Murat became involved in a public scandal following the circulation of a report in which d'Argenson accused the countess of a number of "shocking practices and beliefs," including lesbianism.[15] Although a "lack of information" ini-

14. See, for example, Lewis Seifert, *Fairy Tales, Sexuality and Gender in France: Nostalgic Utopias (1690–1715)*, 149–56.

15. Argenson, *Rapports inédits du lieutenant de police René d'Argenson (1697–1715) publiés d'après les manuscrits conservés à la Bibliothèque Nationale*, 87–88; Robinson, "The Abominable Madame de Murat," 53.

tially prevented the case from going to trial,[16] the accusations nonetheless forced the author to take a temporary hiatus from publishing and
from the worldly society where she had previously been a central fixture.
Estranged from her husband and disinherited by her mother, Murat is
believed to have spent the next year in the Limousin region at the home
of her friend Madame de Nantiat, also exiled from the Parisian social
scene for implications in the same scandal of lesbianism that had affected
Murat.[17] Murat remained there until the late autumn of 1701 when a
police report, dated December 1, 1701, called upon royal authorities to
determine a place of imprisonment for Murat, whose moral debauch-
ery was then confirmed by the fact that the countess was five months
pregnant.[18] Murat was exiled to the Château de Loches in the Touraine
region on April 19, 1702, from which she attempted to escape in March
1706 wearing men's clothing, a hat, and a wig.[19] She was discovered in a
cave beneath a nearby church, and after stabbing and biting the thumb of
the police officers who attempted to arrest her, she was transferred to the
prison at the Château de Saumur and then to the prison at the Château
d'Angers in 1707 before being brought back to Loches later that same
year.[20] Having served the harshest portion of her sentence, Murat was
placed on city arrest and became a regular fixture of provincial society
despite her failing health, the details of which she recorded in a 607-page
journal, framed by a letter to her cousin Mademoiselle de Menou, into
which the countess interpolated poetry, short stories, fairy tales, accounts
of her daily life in exile, and reminiscences of her time in Paris.

In 1709 Murat obtained partial liberty from the Countess d'Argenton
on the condition that she return to the Limousin region and to the home

16. Report follow-up dated February 24, 1700, cited by Cromer, *Édition du Journal pour
Mademoiselle de Menou, d'après le Manuscrit 3471 de la Bibliothèque de l'Arsenal: Ouvrages
de Mme la Comtesse de Murat*, 314.

17. Ibid.; Patard, *Madame de Murat*, 14.

18. Cromer, *Édition du Journal pour Mademoiselle de Menou, d'après le Manuscrit 3471 de
la Bibliothèque de l'Arsenal: Ouvrages de Mme la Comtesse de Murat*, 316, cited by Patard,
Madame de Murat, 14.

19. Boulay de la Meurthe, *Les Prisonniers du roi à Loches sous Louis XIV*, 78, cited by
Patard, *Madame de Murat*, 14.

20. Patard, *Madame de Murat*, 14.

of her aunt, Mademoiselle de Dampierre. It was there that Murat composed her final work, *Les Lutins du Château de Kernosy* (The Sprites of Kernosy Castle; 1710). In this novel, which many consider to be her best work, the ability of individuals, and of nobles in particular, to orchestrate their upward social mobility by manipulating the appearance of supernatural events again becomes a central theme. In this case, a count and a baron use the strategy to win the affections of two young noblewomen living in a solitary château.

After the death of Louis XIV in 1715, the Duke d'Orléans, upon the recommendation of his mistress, Madame de Parbère, invited Murat to return to court. By this time, however, the author was in poor health, riddled with arthritis and swollen with dropsy. She died in her family château of la Buzardière in the province of Maine on September 29, 1716.

Despite her contentious relationship with both the official literary and political establishments, Murat remained a popular and influential author throughout the eighteenth century, with multiple editions of her works appearing every decade until the eve of the French Revolution. *A Trip to the Country* in particular enjoyed significant international acclaim. It was republished at least two more times in Paris during the 1730s and even more frequently abroad. As aristocratic culture came under attack during the tumultuous decades of the French Revolution, however, so also did the novels that memorialized the worldly lifestyle and its values. As a result, there has been no edition of *A Trip to the Country* since 1788, when it was abridged and anthologized in volume 29 of Garnier's *Voyages imaginaires, songes, visions et romans cabalistiques* (Imaginary Voyages, Dreams, Visions and Cabalistic Novels). Due to the lack of available modern editions, combined with the lingering reputation for frivolity, insipidity, long-windedness, and excessive sentimentality associated with novels of this type, today Murat's penultimate novel has been all but forgotten, even by scholars of ancien régime literature.

A Trip to the Country provides an important example of experimental novelistic fiction from the final decades of Louis XIV's reign, a period that extends from 1690 to 1715 and is generally recognized by intellectual historians as encompassing a series of ideological transformations, or shifts in mentalities, that would ultimately pave the way for the dawn of the French Enlightenment. It was during these decades, referred to as "the crisis of European consciousness" in Paul Hazard's seminal 1935 study *The European Mind: The Critical Years, 1680–1715*, that the French, renowned for their relative acceptance of orthodox views throughout the age of absolutism, suddenly began to question all accepted systems, adopting the radical position of Enlightenment doubt within a relatively brief span of time.

This was also a pivotal period of transition for the evolution of the seventeenth-century French novel, a genre whose definition and purpose had been extensively debated since the mid-1600s when proponents of the new short novel (*nouvelle*) had begun arguing for a new aesthetic to replace the heroic adventure novel, or "roman," popular during the earlier part of the century. During the 1660s and 1670s these debates had contributed to a shift in novelistic trends away from long, digressive, anecdotal, and action-oriented works to short, linear, analytical, and psychologically realistic ones, a style epitomized by Lafayette's *La Princesse de Clèves* (The Princess of Clèves; 1678). During the late 1680s, however, a new generation of novelists, dissatisfied with the cultural ramifications of absolutism, took steps to reverse this trend, hearkening back instead to the romanesque predilections of the earlier part of the century, an aesthetically baroque and culturally preabsolutist period in which nobility was perceived as innate and flowery multivolume works such as Honoré d'Urfé's *L'Astrée* (1607–27) and Madeleine de Scudéry's *Clélie* (1654–61) exemplified the dominant novelistic form.

The resurgence in popularity of the romanesque novel, combined with the growing popularity of the new short novel, resulted in what Henri Coulet has referred to as a period of unfocused experimentation, or "confused searching."[21] Although examples of such experimental fiction occur throughout the 1660s and 1670s, they became so popular, particularly between 1690 and 1715, that the trend overtook all other novelistic forms, to the dismay of such contemporary critics as Villiers and Pierre Bayle.[22] While late seventeenth-century hybrid or experimental novels generally retained the shorter length, emphasis on interiority, and use of modern or

---

21. Coulet, *Le Roman jusqu'à la Révolution*, 288.

22. Bayle, *Dictionnaire historique et critique*, 2:833; Villiers, *Entretiens sur les contes de fées, et sur quelques autres ouvrages du temps*, 19–23.

contemporary settings characteristic of the historical novel of the 1660s and 1670s, these elements became infused with seemingly contradictory baroque conventions: short linear plots were infiltrated with digressions recounting extraordinary adventures, psychological exploration and interiority became absorbed into an almost obsessive meditation on individual emotion and sentimentality, and modern historical settings began to serve as a pretext for the interpolation of a variety of short texts drawn from the literary genres deemed fashionable in polite society. Featuring a narrative agenda similar to that of the popular literary magazine the *Mercure Galant,* novels from the turn of the eighteenth century did not seek to illustrate the private motivations behind public events, as the historical novel had done. Rather, novelists sought to elevate private history, and even gossip, to the narrative status of public history, marketing their creations as providing keys to some of the more intriguing contemporary scandals and as secret windows into the private gatherings of the aristocratic elite.

In an effort to make their versions of these events more plausible, turn-of-the-century novelists relied heavily on generic experimentation and hybridization, interpolating a wide variety of subgenres into their novelistic frame narratives with the goal of mimetically reproducing the role that such genres played in the actual social interactions of worldly society in general and of the late seventeenth-century social elite in particular. Some of these interpolated genres, such as literary portraits, letters, short stories, and poems, paid homage to the salon tradition of the earlier part of the century, echoing and revising the style and genres associated with the earlier romance novels of Gautier de La Calprenède, d'Urfé, and Scudéry. Others, such as fairy tales, ghost stories, and proverb plays, represented a quest for novelty and originality, values that would provide the foundation for the French novel's well-documented struggle during the eighteenth century. English Showalter Jr. has attributed this struggle to a desire on the part of a new generation of novelists to represent the individual's emerging subjectivity and place in society, a theme that simultaneously required them to give "a wrench to the forms in vogue."[23] While in the eighteenth century this wrenching produced a variety of

23. Showalter, *The Evolution of the French Novel,* 10.

new novelistic forms, including the epistolary novel, the philosophical tale, the didactic novel, the exotic memoir, and even the confession, at the turn of that century the struggle to find new modes of narration resulted in the production of what Juliette Cherbuliez has described as "hybrid forms that defy generic categorization, as well as longer prose works that echo and revise early romance novels," a type of literary production that she terms "leisure literature."[24] As such, late seventeenth-century novels broke free not only from the political constraints of Louis XIV's classicism but also from the generic constraints of both new and heroic novels, entertaining their public by lending unprecedented importance to the private, independent existence of aristocrats away from the social constraints and pressures of Louis XIV's court and exemplifying a system of values that would later be reprised during the Regency in the early rococo paintings of such artists as Antoine Watteau.

The free-flowing and varied nature of the aristocratic leisure existence foregrounded in such novels as *A Trip to the Country* is far from innocuous politically. By investigating the daily activities of disaffected late seventeenth-century nobles through fictional creations, writers of leisure novels in fact "addressed the changing shapes in French political territory and explored the evolving possibilities for literature as a complex gesture of community."[25] Emerging from a self-conscious political state that invested substantial political and social clout in the dynamic between inclusion and exclusion, novels such as *A Trip to the Country,* which focused unabashedly on the social interactions of those on the margins of court society, were indirectly empowered with a degree of political influence unimaginable in a nonabsolutist setting. Through the use of interpolated texts—including seven ghost stories, seven autobiographical accounts, one literary fairy tale, one rondeau, two gallant poems, two love letters, and eleven proverb comedies, ten of which are appended to the end of the novel and were authored by Murat's salon contemporary and fellow fairy-tale author Catherine Bédacier Durand—*A Trip to the Country* in fact takes an inventory of the disparate material and discursive spaces that remain free from absolutist control. The framing of these

---

24. Cherbuliez, *The Place of Exile,* 22.
25. Ibid., 15.

narratives, plays, and poems into a novel that details a trip to a country estate taken by the novel's seven main characters allows the genre to "order these spaces into a coherent whole,"[26] creating an imaginary sphere evocative of the earlier salon but that in transforming the physical space of the salon into a diasporic community of like-minded individuals, resists the spatial and geographical control of movement perpetuated by the monarchy through the political institution of exile. Leisure literature defied the monarchy by "imagining and interrogating the viability of a world beyond authority's reach."[27] As such, it became a form of everyday political engagement with absolutism's culture of exclusion.

One of the most striking aspects of the novel's historical frame narrative, set in Paris and its surrounding countryside between the end of the War of the League of Augsburg (1688–97) and the beginning of the War of Spanish Succession (1701–14), is the marked absence of contemporary references to Versailles or to Louis XIV. As the narrator attests, one of the chief beauties of the fictional estate where the characters decide to spend the summer is that in addition to being only a day's drive from Paris, the Count de Selincourt's château is surrounded by "pleasantly shaded woods, which the rays of the sun have difficulty penetrating." The "pleasantly shaded woods," which the characters embrace as a welcome alternative to the "rays of the sun," is only the first of many indications that the society the novel represents is both politically and culturally autonomous, as untouched by the influence of the Sun King as the forest floor is shaded from the heat of the day.

The freedom from monarchical influence is not limited to the characters' geographical isolation, however. Curiously, although the novel takes place in France between 1697 and 1699, the centralized court of Versailles is only alluded to on two occasions: when the Count de Selincourt and the Marquis de Brésy recount stories of how, in their younger years, they had to choose between attending court functions or remaining in Paris with their love interests. While Brésy's decision to go to Versailles adds stress to his love relationship with Madame d'Ardanne, Selincourt's decision to forego the king's bedtime ceremony (*le coucher*) causes him to make great headway with the reluctant Madame de Sardise.

26. Ibid., 35.
27. Ibid., 15.

It is likely that the Countess de Murat drew her primary inspiration for the country setting and festive pastimes of the fictional Château de Selincourt from those of her own intimate circle of friends at the time of the novel's publication. Indeed, several of the characters' names and attributes recall the more prominent members of Murat's literary entourage. The surname of Madame d'Orselis, for example, likely presents an anagram of either "Courcelles" or "La Force," referring either to the prominent salonnière Anne-Thérèse de Marguenat de Courcelles, Marquise de Lambert, whose salon Murat frequented or to Murat's cousin Charlotte-Rose Caumont de la Force. The surname of the Marquise d'Arcire similarly appears to be an anagram of "Bédacier," referring to the author's close friend Catherine Bédacier Durand, who authored the proverb comedies that appeared at the end of the novel's original 1699 edition and subsequent early eighteenth-century editions.

Unlike earlier novels, however, which largely portray châteaux where nobles spend their exile as understated anticourts—places of solitude and reflection, as in the depiction of the Château de Coulommiers in *La Princesse de Clèves*—*A Trip to the Country* consistently seeks to establish Selincourt as the modern equivalent of Versailles, appropriating the earlier court's most prominent ideological signifiers in terms of both ceremony and decor. Like Versailles, Selincourt is furnished with an orangery, a labyrinth, and an immense park leading down to a large body of water, the walkways of which are adorned with marble statues. Here, however, rather than destabilizing, intimidating, and overwhelming those in their presence, as was the goal of such spaces at Versailles, the gardens of Selincourt provide important opportunities for liberty and privacy. As such, Murat's novel recalls d'Aulnoy's inscription of elements of Versailles in her fairy tales and especially the use of Saint-Cloud, the château of Louis XIV's brother and his wife, the Princess Palatine, as a frame narrative for one of her volumes of fairy tales.[28]

Even more astonishing is the degree to which the *fêtes galantes* ("gallant festivals") enjoyed by the characters at Selincourt directly recall André Félibien's descriptions of parties hosted by Louis XIV during the 1660s and 1670s. Boat rides by candlelight accompanied by musicians, exotic delicacies prepared by unseen hands, and lavishly decorated out-

28. For more on this, see Duggan, *Salonnières, Furies, and Fairies,* 227–30.

door balls abound. This time, however, the instigators of such revelry are aristocrats, not monarchs, and the power structure being performed is republican rather than absolutist: everyone must take a turn at organizing and overseeing the gallant entertainments, and everyone has the opportunity to evaluate their success. Even the crucial element of surprise is revised and reappropriated by the seven main characters, transforming the *roi magicien* ("magician king"), who used such tactics to assert his absolute political dominance over the court and over the nation, into a *fée-enchanteur* ("fairy enchanter"), a chivalric lord or lady in the service of his or her fellow aristocrats, as in the *fête galante* that Selincourt organizes for the Marquise d'Arcire, to the delight of the entire group.

In refashioning the monarch's monopoly over court spectacle, the novel also rejects his monopoly over the organization of daily court activities and leisure. Rather than waking at dawn or cutting short their evening festivities to assist in the *lever* or *coucher* of the king, the characters at Selincourt rise very late and go to bed when they please. Similarly, although the Count de Selincourt occasionally organizes for his guests a trip to the opera or a hunting expedition, the responsibility of staving off boredom is ultimately shared equally among the company, with activities decided in conjunction with the rules of variety, novelty, and public opinion rather than in accordance with a preestablished schedule. Under this alternative court existence, the king's most ideologically charged diversions are similarly revamped, not surprisingly with an element of satire. The only hunting scene in *A Trip to the Country* culminates not with the requisite portrait of the king and his entourage posing around the spectacle of a fallen stag but rather with a heroic rescue executed by the Marquis de Brésy, who rushes to the aid of the female narrator in true knightly fashion after the narrator is thrown from her horse, her bouffant hair having entangled itself around a tree branch. Similarly, the typical evening theater production is transformed from a passive spectacle, in which the courtiers watch while the play is performed on a proscenium stage, into a proverb comedy, a humorous interactive production varying in length from one scene to several acts that, to quote Perry Gethner's description, "illustrates a well-known proverb without using the proverb in the text; in the end the audience has to guess."[29]

---

29. Gethner, "Playful Wit in Salon Games," 225.

Finally, and perhaps most striking, is the way in which the characters overtly reinvent the social hierarchy that ordered and regulated the court dynamic under Louis XIV. Unlike at Versailles, where one's social status in relation to the king became a key determinant of one's inclusion and importance, at Selincourt talent and wit replace rank as the most valued asset. Those who display the ability to amuse, to entertain, and, most importantly, to impress the other courtiers with their stories quickly become integral cofashioners of the court's most privileged inner circle, while those who fail to do so are categorically banished. Such is the case with the visiting neighbors, who fail to appreciate the ingenuity of a literary fairy tale, and with the unfortunate Madame de Talemonte, who is unable to match the central narrator story for story and thus returns to Paris in disgrace. Selincourt's nonconformity to the monarch's rules of social inclusion prevalent at Versailles does not limit itself to a blatant disregard for differences of rank among aristocrats, however. At Versailles, bourgeois ministers were often accepted on the basis of their loyalty to the absolutist enterprise. At Selincourt, however, bourgeois who seek to prove their loyalty to the aristocratic lifestyle are only tolerated long enough to serve as fodder for ridicule. Such is the case with the comical Richard/de Richardin family, whom the aristocratic characters visit out of boredom and then mock in a scathing proverb comedy. The humiliation of these characters in particular evokes the mocking of the bourgeois Monsieur de la Dandinardière in the frame narrative of d'Aulnoy's last two volumes of fairy tales.

In refusing to acknowledge Versailles' domination over late seventeenth-century aristocratic culture and in appropriating for themselves the aging monarch's monopoly over the creation of political signifiers and spectacular court festivities, the aristocrats of *A Trip to the Country* ultimately elevate themselves and their society to a level of importance tantamount to that of the monarch himself, using Louis XIV's most important tools of absolutist propaganda for the promotion of their own values, lifestyle, and projected political power. In denying Versailles its current status as the center of aristocratic French culture and in asserting Selincourt—a decentralized, merit-based, free-spirited court—as the new aristocratic political model, Murat's novel thus lays important ideological groundwork for the Enlightenment of the century to come in addition to breaking with the centralized, absolutist regime of the present.

In breaking with Louis XIV's classicism, Murat's text also breaks with the fairy-tale tradition established by d'Aulnoy and her fellow *conteuses* ("storytellers") throughout the 1690s in two important ways. First, in featuring a fairy tale that promotes a relationship between nobility and merit, Murat reverses a trend in fairy-tale production from the first vogue in which the marvelous supernatural serves to reinforce essentialist notions of aristocratic identity. Second, in replacing the fairy tale with the ghost story as the most common interpolated narrative in her hybrid experimental novel, Murat radicalizes the critical potential of the marvelous supernatural employed by her predecessors, reintegrating both the existence of supernatural events and the critique of society implicit in these events with the natural reality of Murat's late seventeenth-century public. As Max Lüthi has described, the difference between the marvelous supernatural prevalent in fairy tales and the fantastic supernatural typical of ghost stories is the level of dimensionality on which the supernatural operates. In fairy tales, the constant presence of magic as a norm causes the natural and supernatural to function in a one-dimensional relationship, signaling to the reader that the fairy-tale world occupies a separate plane of existence. In ghost stories, by contrast, the intervention of the supernatural constitutes an exceptional occurrence, intervening in the natural world in a two-dimensional manner and signaling to the reader that the world in which the ghost story takes place operates on the same plane of existence as the readers' everyday reality.[30] In refusing to remove the social institutions challenged by her ghost stories from the natural world, Murat's critique of contemporary social institutions thus surpasses those of her fairy-tale predecessors, engaging directly with the reality of absolutist France while pushing the limits of this reality in unprecedented new directions. As such, *A Trip to the Country* paves the way for the powerful and direct critique of social institutions that would take place during the French Enlightenment.

---

30. Lüthi, *The European Folktale,* 4–10.

A Note on the Translation

This translation follows the original 1699 edition as closely as possible, referring to the 1734 edition and to the 1788 editions for consultation only in moments when clarification due to typographical or punctuation errors was needed. At times when typographical errors had the potential to change the meaning of a passage, we made an educated guess based on our own understanding of the text and on the decisions of later editors. These decisions are clarified in the footnotes.

The goal of our translation is to strike a balance between Eugene Nida's principle of equivalent effect[1] and our desire to preserve the reader's awareness of the text as a cultural and historical artifact. Since the language of the late seventeenth-century text would have been close to the vernacular of its original readers, we have striven to cultivate a style and tone that is easy for the modern Anglophone reader to understand and that retains, to the greatest degree possible, the lively, readable, and enjoyable qualities appreciated by the novel's original readers. In keeping with our desire for readability, we have added quotation marks to frame dialogue, a practice not current at the time. We have also added bracketed stage directions to the interpolated proverb comedy.

In the interest of conserving the modern reader's awareness of the text as a cultural and historical artifact, we have chosen to stay as close to the word choice and syntax of the original edition as possible, retaining cognates, calques, and markers of the original French as signs of foreignness, prioritizing mild archaisms over modern-sounding words, and reserving contractions only for passages of informality or heightened emotion. We

---

1. Nida, *Toward a Science of Translation*, 159.

retain the nonstop sentences of the original and eighteenth-century editions of the novel almost ubiquitously, substituting periods for colons or semicolons only in cases where the early modern punctuation obscures the meaning of the passage for the modern reader. In the interest of preserving the materiality of the original edition, we retain original paragraph structures except in cases where a paragraph break in the original edition appears to have been made in error.[2] The wide spaces that appear before the interpolated fairy tale, interpolated verse poetry, and epistolary fragments within the body of the text reflect the materiality of the 1699 edition, as does the use of italic print wherever present.

In the three instances where rhymed verse poetry is interpolated into the work, our translation prioritizes the form and structure of the original poem. In cases where multiple translations of a single word are possible, we have offered varying definitions based on our interpretation of the word's context. The problem of navigating the opposition between *tu* and *vous* was not an issue in this translation, since the aristocratic main characters only make use of the second-person singular when addressing their servants.

Titles of nobility have been translated except for "Chevalier," which has no English equivalent. Similarly, we have translated direct addresses such as "Monsieur le duc" as "Sir," since the English equivalent "His (or Your) Lordship the Duke" indicates an address to one's superior rather than a gesture of respect to someone older, the manner in which such addresses are employed in the text. Symbols such as "***" or "..." that often substitute for proper names in the original have similarly been retained and have been standardized to three periods or asterisks.

2. In two instances, the original edition contains paragraph breaks that occur in the middle of a word or a sentence.

A Trip to the Country
by Henriette-Julie de Castelnau, Comtesse de Murat

Portrait of Henriette-Julie de Castelnau, Countess de Murat, by Jacques Harrewyn (engraving, 9×12, signed). Paris, Bibliothèque Nationale de France (N2 MURAT, 55A7037).

To Her Most Serene Highness
The Dowager Princess of Conty[1]

RONDEAU[2]

Cupid is great; his mother[3] *resembles you:*
Go from Versailles to her isle;[4] *you'll see that it's true.*
On the roads crowds will be scattered far and wide,
Bringing you incense and hearts from every side.
As myth the other Venus will be dismissed.
I've never lied; believe me now in this;
Come learn about the character and bliss
Of those who, marching behind love's banner, cried:
  Cupid is great.
On just one point does the resemblance cease:
You have the goddess's charming qualities,
Such as her beauty, bearing, gentle looks and grace;
But in your heart passion for Mars holds no place,
Nor for Adonis,[5] *or the other mysteries*
  Of Cupid the great.

---

1. Marie-Anne de Bourbon (1666–1739), who was the daughter of Louis XIV and Louise de la Vallière and the widow of Louis-Armand, Prince of Conti, was Murat's patron. Murat also dedicated her first volume of fairy tales, published in 1698, to the Princess of Conti.

2. The choice of this type of poem, which was considered archaic by the end of the seventeenth century, pays homage to the worldly, gallant, "precious" salon culture that dominated aristocratic society prior to Louis XIV's personal reign.

3. In this hyperbolic address, the princess is compared to Venus, model of beauty and mother of Cupid.

4. The reference is to the Greek island of Cythera, mythological home to Venus.

5. Adonis, a hunter of remarkable beauty, and Mars, god of war, figured among Venus's lovers.

A Trip to the Country

{ PART ONE }

*Y*ou ask me, madam, for the story[6] of the trip that I took to Selincourt;[7] I found it too agreeable for its recollection not to give me pleasure; my only fear is to make it too long; but since you desire an exact account, I am obliged, with your permission, to follow the example of our novelists,[8] acquainting you with the conversations that we had and with the stories that were recounted there.

We left Paris at the beginning of this summer, the Marquise d'Arcire, Madame d'Orselis, and myself, to go and spend two months at the Count de Selincourt's estate: peacetime leaving our warriors the leisure to take some rest, nothing seems to them more fresh and more appealing than the pleasures of the countryside. You are aware, madam, that this estate owes one of its greatest beauties to the river Seine, on the banks of which it is situated: you are also not unaware that it has magnificent avenues, impressive fountains, beautiful gardens, pleasantly shaded woods, which the rays of the sun have difficulty penetrating, and that the apartments of the château are superb, as much for their size as for the furniture that

6. The French term *récit* designated a true narrative that recounts events of recent occurrence. In the seventeenth century, there were several types of *récits,* including the *récit exact* ("exact account"), which the correspondent requests, and the *long récit* ("long account"), which connoted boredom and which the narrator hopes to avoid.

7. At the turn of the eighteenth century, the Selincourt seigneury belonged to the family of Charles-Nicolas Manessier, Viscount de Selincourt, an infantry captain in the king's army. The château, which had been destroyed in a fire, was not rebuilt until 1734. Although in the context of Murat's novel the estate is only a day's drive from Paris by carriage, it is in fact located more than 99 miles (160 kilometers) away in Picardy.

8. The traditions alluded to are those of Madeleine de Scudéry, Marie-Madeleine Pioche de la Vergne (Countess de Lafayette), and Marie-Catherine Desjardins (Madame de Villedieu), who in their romances and psychological novels made extensive use of detailed transcription of conversations and interpolated stories.

decorates them. You will remember, madam, that the dinners held there are refined and well executed and that order shines everywhere in this sumptuous locale: but one thing that you will not perhaps remember, even though you knew it better than another, is that the count is very likable; that he has long, blond, naturally curly hair, the prodigious quantity of which goes down to his belt; that he has a pleasant face; and that his countenance is gallant and noble; as for wit, he has an infinite amount of it; but he tends to dominate conversations a little too much; he does not give adequate consideration to the opinions of others; he only shines in response to his own; he speaks too loudly, decides reputations too freely: always persuaded that one cannot be mistaken in judging things in the worst possible light, he scarcely acknowledges virtue, except for the kind that is too ostentatious; his moods are unpredictable; one moment he is moralistic to the most severe extreme, and the next he is astonishingly permissive; other times, excessively cheerful, he lapses suddenly into a state of sadness so profound that it only furnishes him with dismal thoughts: nonetheless, his appeal is infinite.

There was a time, madam, when these praises accompanied by the truths that follow them would not have been to your taste; you would have insisted upon a portrait without shadow: today I must include these same truths, to make you tolerate what I say in his favor.

Because I have begun to present portraits,[9] I must provide you with an overview of all the actors in the scene.

The Marquise d'Arcire is beautiful, young, witty, and gentle.

A longer portrait would bore you, and perhaps, wishing to forget that Selincourt was an unfaithful lover, you will remember only too well that the countess[10] is a preferred rival.

---

9. Literally "because I have begun to paint." In using a visual portrait-painting metaphor to present the portraits of her main characters, the narrator situates her text specifically in the tradition of salon-inspired seventeenth-century literary portraiture. The collection by Anne-Marie Louise d'Orléans, Duchess de Montpensier, of verbal portraits (1659), for example, similarly relies on metaphors associated with painted portraiture.

10. This reference to a character not named in the text calls attention to the volatile nature of love and friendship in late seventeenth-century worldly, aristocratic society, the backdrop against which *A Trip to the Country* is set.

Madame d'Orselis is a beautiful woman, in every feature;[11] she even has a lot of wit, but her temperament has much in common with that of the count, and if Cupid had ever been inclined to unite the two of them, their conversations would have appeared more militaristic than amorous.

As for me, madam, I do not judge it necessary to paint myself; you know me too well, and my story, the abridged version of which I shall recount, will provide all the necessary overview of my person. When we arrived at Selincourt, the count had with him the Chevalier de Chanteuil: he has beautiful brown hair, a slender figure, large eyes from which fire emanates as if they were ablaze, teeth like pearls, honor and probity, appealing wit, a consistent and gentle disposition, and love affairs that are always passionate, and often brief; but no matter how unfaithful he may be, his moderation makes him give considerate treatment to the abandoned mistress as much as to the current favorite.

The Duke de . . . , uncle of Selincourt, who is an elderly well-mannered lord and who happened to be visiting the count at the time, made it acceptable for the ladies to stay;[12] and at first we thought of nothing but our own amusement. We followed our hosts down the avenues; we went down to a grated door, which looked out onto the park; all the fountains were at play. The sun had just set; it is, in my opinion, the most beautiful moment of the day: there is not a single tiny flower that does not emit a lovely scent, and not a bird that does not sing; even one's thoughts find themselves more at liberty than during the noonday heat.

After having walked to the point of exhaustion, we passed over bridges that cross great moats full of swiftly running water to return to the château; each person chose an apartment; for myself, I insisted upon a lovely room, which looks out over the most pleasant ornamental pond[13] in the

---

11. An alternative translation of the word *trait* is "stroke," a term used to describe the realization of a painted portrait. This play on words is further reinforced by the second part of the expression: "*pour trait*," a homonym of the modern French word "portrait," which would have been spelled "*pourtrait*" at the turn of the seventeenth century.

12. The duke acts as a chaperon for the three unmarried women, whose extended visit to Selincourt would otherwise have provoked social scrutiny.

13. The expression "*parterre d'eau*" refers specifically to a series of pools enclosed in stone and connected by canals. These ponds often took the shape of scrolls or shells and were separated from one another by intervening spaces of gravel or turf. At Versailles,

world. The count was, that day, as handsome as Cupid, and as smitten as
a Spaniard: the marquise let the joy in her eyes shine freely, the cause of
which was not unknown to any of us. Constraint[14] was banished. After
supper we returned down the path to the gardens: our lovers had the
pleasure of conversing with one another for an hour; and the chevalier
lost his freedom in even less time at the side of the beautiful Orselis.
There was no one, not even the old duke, who did not want to engage in
amorous pursuit. I was without a partner; and thus by compassion or by
inclination, he told me flattering things in the manner of the old court,[15]
which could have been effective, if I had seen him only in the dark.

After having taken a few turns separated in this manner, we rejoined
one another around a great fountain, the banks of which were carpeted
with grass: the conversation became general; we discussed a variety of
subjects; finally, without realizing it, we fell upon the choices we had
made of the apartments we wished to occupy. "In my opinion," I said,
"mine seems the best situated: I am separated from everyone: I can only
be awakened gently by the sound of the water and the song of the birds,
and if I cannot sleep, nothing is more suitable for inspiring pleasant day-
dreams." "Indeed," said the count, "but what if I told you that spirits are
often heard in that room, and that those who have slept there for one
night could not wait to leave it the next day?" "I should answer you,"
I replied, "in the same manner that an illustrious lady once did when
placed in a similar situation, and perhaps I might even match the courage
she exhibited at the time." Everyone wished to know the identity of the
lady and the rest of the story.

"Because you have requested it," I replied, "I shall recount it to you:[16]

---

such ponds were arranged geometrically and were strategically placed to amplify the château's magnificent facade.

14. In choosing this word, Murat expressly differentiates the relaxed social ambiance of
Selincourt from that of the court at Versailles, where daily routines were highly codified
and ritualized.

15. This refers to Louis XIV's court at Versailles prior to the king's secret marriage to the
Marquise of Maintenon in 1683, at which point the gallant, festive ambiance increasingly
gave way to a tone of piety and austerity.

16. This apparently true story about the late poet Antoinette du Ligier de la Garde
Deshoulières (1638–94) also appears in the first published biography of her, written by

I learned it from Madame Deshoulières herself, to whom the event occurred: she went to see one of her friends, a woman of the nobility,[17] who lived on an estate about fifteen or twenty leagues[18] from Paris: she was offered her choice of any bedroom in the house, with the exception of one where, it was said, strange things could be heard, and it was believed that the mother of the master, who had been dead for a year, was causing all the noisy commotion: this was exactly the sort of adventure that Madame Deshoulières had been seeking for a long time; the sharpness of her mind caused her to be somewhat skeptical of everything that is said about this subject. No matter how hard they tried to remind her of her present condition, for she was pregnant, she remained adamant in her desire to see the ghost and would not even allow one of her maidservants to sleep in the adjoining dressing room.[19] She was pitied, she was criticized; but she had to be served according to her wishes. The bedroom in question was large and vast, the thresholds of the windows were deep and the fireplace was antiquated: she climbed into bed, had a roaring fire lit, and had a large candle placed on a candlestick (the word 'candle'[20] does not belong to noble vocabulary, but the circumstance is essential to the storyline): and taking out a book, as was her custom, she told the woman who was

---

Guillaume de la Boissière de Chambors and prefaced to the collection of her and her daughter's complete works: *Oeuvres de Mme et de Mlle Deshoulières: Nouvelle édition, augmentée de leur éloge historique et de plusieurs pièces qui n'avoient pas encore été imprimés* (Paris: David l'aîné, 1747).

17. Translations of this story by nineteenth-century American women writers state that Deshoulières went to visit the Count and Countess de Lunéville (Starling, "Singular Adventure of Madame Deshoulières," 317; Nowell, "A Ghost Story by May Mannering," 400).

18. A league is approximately 3.1 miles (5 kilometers).

19. A typical aristocratic apartment was composed of an antechamber, a main bedroom, a dressing room, and a cabinet (a small reading room or private study). Servants customarily slept in both the dressing room and the antechamber not only to be close at hand in case of an emergency but also in order to guard the clothes, jewelry, and other valuables typically consigned to the dressing room.

20. The use of this word would have been considered unacceptable in more refined genres of poetry. In including it, the narrator explicitly prioritizes realistic everyday language over arbitrary poetic statutes, such as those imposed by the royally sponsored French Academy.

serving her to close the door firmly: this was done. Having finished her reading, she put out her light and fell asleep. Just barely had she begun to taste the charms of slumber when she was awakened by a noise at the very same door: the door opened, something entered the room with heavy footsteps; Madame Deshoulières called out to it that she could not be made afraid; that if someone was trying to scare her, it was in vain; that she was resolved to shed light on the spirit's identity. No matter how much she talked, no one responded; the mysterious being continued to approach and it even rudely overturned the large, ill-perched folding screen at the foot of her bed in such a way that the curtains, the rings of which were very wide and which passed through very delicate rods, made an ear-shattering crash, which would have terrified anyone except our heroine: but she swore afterward that her heart did not even skip a beat.

She continued to harangue the spirit, whom she believed to be some love-struck servant; but the silent ghost did not utter a word; on the contrary, moving into the space between her bed and the wall, it over-turned the night table, which, since it was very tall and the candlestick that was on top of it very heavy, crashed down with a frightening clatter; this clatter was followed by a small agitation that the ghost gave to the candlestick, rattling it against the tiles of the bedroom; the duration of this action seemed interminable; finally, weary of so much exertion, it came and leaned against the foot of the bed: it was at this moment that Madame Deshoulières showed her courage. 'Aha!' she cried, 'I will find out who you are, because you have come so close to me!' Then, reaching out with both hands into the place where she had heard the specter, she seized upon two very hairy ears, which she resolved to keep hold of until daybreak to shed light on the mystery: never was there anything so docile as the owner of these ears, never was there anyone so patient as Madame Deshoulières; for the nights were extremely long and the position un-comfortable, and it was not until the first light of dawn that she perceived the spirit to be a large housedog named Grosblanc,[21] a good creature if there ever was one, who, far from wishing her ill-will for having held him down for such a long time, licked her hands to thank her for it: she burst out laughing, sent Grosblanc to sleep on some chairs, and closed her eyes

21. "Grosblanc" translates literally as "Fat White."

with eagerness. The master and the mistress of the house had not slept a wink all night long: the idea of a pregnant woman given over to frightening apparitions had shaken them up so cruelly that they rose early to verify she was not dead, or at least that she had not given birth. The good people opened the door very gently and almost did not dare to speak, for fear that she might take offense to their boldness: but Madame Deshoulières, opening the bed curtains, presented them with a face so gay that they began by telling her that she was more fortunate than wise to have emerged from such a great peril unscathed. She responded by giving them a very eloquent account of what had happened to her: the hair on their heads was standing on end when, presenting them with Grosblanc, she said to the husband: 'See, see, it is Grosblanc whom you have taken for so long to be the ghost of your esteemed mother. Here is the cause of so much alarm.' The gentleman looked at his wife and his dog, ashamed, speechless, not knowing whether to get angry or to laugh: but Madame Deshoulières had a certain firmness of character that made her think like a man of reason and good breeding. 'No, no, sir,' she said to him, 'you will not remain in error any further; I see that your misapprehension is dear to you: you cannot bring yourself to believe a truth that destroys an illusion that has held power over you for so long: but I will complete my work, and I will make you see,' she added, 'that all that happened last night came of natural causes.' Then, getting up, she went to examine the door, the catch to which was so poorly wrought that even though it had been locked, the least amount of movement was sufficient to open it: 'you may see already,' she continued, 'why Grosblanc, who apparently does not like to sleep outdoors, chose this room rather than another; the rest is easy to imagine: he found the folding screen, he threw it on my bed, the night table fell by the same chance; Grosblanc took a liking to the candlestick, and knocking over the candle solely in order to detach it, he wished to come up onto the bed, but first he asked my permission; and there you have,' she added in conclusion, 'an example of how trifles often pass for matters of importance.'"

That, madam, is how I concluded the story of Madame Deshoulières, which was found heroic on her part and very amusing on the part of Grosblanc. "It is in this way," said Madame d'Orselis, "that the majority of apparitions turn out when one looks into them more deeply." "How-

ever," responded the marquise, "I have heard talk of a gentleman from
the area near Blois, whose ancestor walks habitually about the avenues
and gardens around his château, and who often shows himself in the windows." "You are doubtlessly speaking of Monsieur de Donnery," added
the chevalier. "He is my relative, and I have heard it told a hundred times
that everyone from masters to servants is so accustomed to seeing this
spirit, who, by the way, has never harmed anyone, that they are not afraid
of it in the least: nothing has been spared to bring him to rest: but, seeing
his resistance, it was finally decided that he should be left to inhabit the
château La Sourdière;²² that is the name of the estate."

  "Oh, really!" said the Duke de . . . . "If we are going to tell ghost stories, I will tell you one of the best. Are you familiar with that of La Motte
Thibergeau?" he added. "The family is very old and well known in the
region of Vendôme or Anjou; I no longer remember which of these two
provinces.²³ It is said that a youngest son²⁴ by this name, being ready to
go off to battle, and having no money to furnish the necessary horses and
servants, was informed by some peasants that a certain château, which
had the reputation of being inhabited by devils, had belonged to his
forefathers; that it had only been abandoned because of the ravages that
the devils were making of it, and that it was believed to contain some
hidden treasure. A youngest son without money would have heeded an
even more far-fetched account: Thibergeau did not doubt the truth of
this one, and resolved to spend a night in this old château. He took two
pistols and a good sword, had a fire made and some torches lit; sending
away the servant who had done all of these services for him, he remained,
seated on an uncomfortable chair, which he had had brought into a large
hall apt to frighten anyone due to its dilapidated state. As soon as night
fell, he saw two tall lackeys enter, well dressed in the livery of his house,
who were holding a large basket and who laid out place settings on an
elegant table laden with food; the dishes were light, but numerous, and

22. The Château La Sourdière is located in Poitou-Charentes, in the commune of Châ-
teauneuf.

23. Built in the early seventeenth century, the Château La Motte Thibergeau is indeed
located between Vendôme and Anjou, near the town of Flée.

24. Due to the principle of primogeniture determining aristocratic inheritance, only the
oldest son would inherit the family estate.

decorated with the coat of arms of Thibergeau's family. Watching out of the corner of his eye to see what all the fuss would lead to, he saw three distinguished-looking men enter, one dressed in blue and the other two in red: they sat down at the table, deep in silence, and began to eat heartily. One among them, turning toward our adventurer, said to him: 'Come have supper, Thibergeau.' 'I am not hungry, sir,' Thibergeau replied. 'Oh, come on! Don't make us force you,' added one of the men in red. 'It is fasting time,' replied the youngest son, who was beginning to become quite frightened and who was discreetly arming himself, from time to time, with the sign of the cross. '*Come, come, Thibergeau,*' added the third, '*Twice the fast, twice the portion*':[25] this, my ladies, is where the proverb originates. Thibergeau, though so forcefully invited, nevertheless refused again. He was left in peace for the remainder of the supper, and when the table was cleared, one of these extraordinary men said: 'Follow us, or you might be sorry.' Thibergeau's legs were as weak as his appetite, but he summoned all his courage and resolved to obey. He followed them down to the cellar, where the phantoms disappeared with a thundering crash. Thibergeau had his servants rummage about in the place where the apparition had vanished and found treasures of infinite value and tableware made of silver and vermilion, of which some of the plates have even been kept in his house to give more weight to the account: it passes for a solid truth in the province; and if it is merely a legend, there is not another backed by more persuading circumstances: there was even an authentically rendered parliamentary decree, awarding the silver serving pieces to Thibergeau, after his older brothers had demanded their share from him."

The duke stopped at these words. "In truth, Duke," I said to him, "you scared me! I find Thibergeau even more courageous than Madame Deshoulières: but she has her sex in her favor, which well augments her bravery." It was so late when I finished speaking that the company parted ways and decided to retire to their beds; I will tell you in passing, madam, that I heard nothing the entire night, and that if spirits ordinarily haunt

25. This popular proverb, which dates from the Middle Ages, was commonly recited during Lent, a period during which fasting was required on Ash Wednesday and also on Fridays.

this bedroom, I apparently did not seem worthy of their wrath. We awoke very late the next morning and dined sumptuously in the neighboring orangery,[26] where fountains kept the air cool and fresh. The Duke de . . . , Madame d'Orselis, and the chevalier took up a game of hombre,[27] while the count and the marquise conversed, apparently about their passion: I watched the card game, and I noticed that Chanteuil was highly favoring Madame d'Orselis, and was allowing her to win as easily as he could. Afterward, we all got into a carriage to take a stroll along the banks of the river.

We saw a boat covered with leaves and honeysuckle branches that was there solely to greet us: on board we found stools to sit upon comfortably, and refreshments; another boat followed behind with the oboists in the employ of the count. You are aware, madam, that he has some very good players and that the oboe is of all instruments the most pleasant upon the water. We did not board until it was time to have supper; and the group found itself augmented by a man of whom you know so little that it is fitting to present you his portrait.

He is tall and a bit plump, although young; he has beautiful legs and the airs of a young courtier: impertinent, proud, reckless; he wears a brown wig, he has large, black eyes, beautiful to perfection, a somewhat aquiline nose, and a rather large mouth, although red and pleasant; he has the most beautiful teeth in the world: he has adorned his mind with everything that came easily to him: he is naturally witty, and has an even greater imagination: since his head is full of comedy, opera and verse, he quotes passages accurately and knows so well how to use these talents to his advantage, that one can never be bored in his presence. What can I say, madam? The Marquis de Brésy is a very likable man, and his arrival delighted everyone. "My heavens, my friend," he said to the count upon entering, "here is the attraction of good company; how different I find

26. A garden composed of orange trees. After wintering indoors, the trees were brought outdoors in containers and arranged symmetrically, as was fashionable at Versailles.

27. This Spanish card game, literally translated as "The Man," can accommodate between two and five players. Although gambling was a popular pastime of the late seventeenth-century elite, it also had a sinister aspect: Louis XIV encouraged it to bankrupt and immobilize the nobility at court.

this place from the tents[28] we inhabited in previous years; and provided that these ladies do not take aversion to me, I will not leave until they do." Selincourt welcomed him with open arms, and the marquise received quite favorable glances from him; she is not a flirt; he would have lavished his gazes on her in vain, if the count, by the effect of some whim unknown to any of us at the time, had not chosen to speak to me a few days later in a different tone from the usual. I did not pay any attention to it at first; then, my experience of the world could not but make me aware that though he was not in love with me, he at least wanted to make me believe so; for during the next few days he treated me with the kind of care and attention not reserved for those to whom one feels indifference. I am a friend of the marquise: this situation embarrassed me. "If I go," I said to myself, "and reveal this secret to Madame d'Arcire, she will reproach her lover; he will find me indiscreet or vain; he will hate me, and once discord has pervaded our thoughts, we will each go our separate ways: and it will be said in high society that women cannot live together." I concluded from this little reasoning that it was up to the marquise to perceive the coquetry of her lover, and that I should listen to the count's claims of affection without believing them, but without rebuffing them. This is a middle ground difficult to stake out, but since I remained self-possessed, I succeeded at it perfectly. On the other hand, Brésy, unaware of all of our romantic interests and not being in the mood to take great pains over women, continued to indulge his initial inclination to want to please the marquise; and the marquise, on her end, having perceived all too well the efforts that Selincourt was making on my behalf, found it more convenient to listen to a likable man who fussed over her, than to reproach a lover who wanted to abandon her; perhaps Brésy was more to her taste; perhaps she also hoped to lure back her unfaithful lover by such behavior: he would not be the first to have been called back by this secret.

The chevalier and Madame d'Orselis already seemed to be forging a romantic attachment: she held back at this early phase, revealing only the brilliance of her wit to her new admirer, who was enchanted by it. He, for his part, advanced his cause considerably by showing only his enthu-

---

28. Allusion to the military tents where officers such as Brésy and Selincourt, as members of the sword nobility, would have spent their summers during combat.

siasm and saving his fickleness for another season: and you may well see, madam, that they were misleading one another. The duke continued to say tender things to me, without any respect for his nephew, who was not really frightened by this rival; he was proposing some fairly solid things, however, and if one's heart had felt just a little interest, one could have gotten him to go much further.

A few days after the Marquis de Brésy had arrived, we went walking in a neighboring forest; there we came upon a magnificent buffet laid out under a leafy shelter; the oboists came to join us. I was not in love with the count, and I strongly believed that he was not very much in love with me; but since his preference for me flattered my vanity, the very appearance of it was sufficient for me, and I was that day in a joyful mood that, I dare say, did not make me a boring companion. Selincourt, even though he was at fault, began to become enraged by the love affair that he believed to be developing between Madame d'Arcire and the marquis: he increased his attentions to me twofold; but, to speak frankly, he was more animated by his jealousy than by my beauty. The marquise, who had one lover to retain and one to win back, was not without occupation: cunning was necessary to succeed at both these enterprises, and she had never before exhibited so much. As for Brésy, he had only one objective: but he seemed so intent upon it that he appeared all too amusing.

The old duke, who wanted to appear attractive to me, lavished me, so to speak, with flattery and politeness; and while the chevalier and the beautiful Orselis hardly gave a thought to the rest of us, they seemed so happy that we had the urge to follow their example.

In this kind of ambiance, you can be sure, madam, that the conversation did not flag: there were, at the start, some stinging remarks couched in sweetness, which permitted only responses in the same tone; but at the end of the meal, the count kissed my hand, having received the strawberries he had requested from me. The marquise said to me, while laughing, that I was apparently like Madame de . . . of whom Monsieur de Bussy[29]

---

29. In the cruel portrait that he writes about his cousin the Marquise de Sevigné in his novel *Histoire Amoureuse des Gaules* (1660), Bussy-Rabutin declares that she let everyone kiss her hands, either because she did not find them beautiful or because she found this custom too common to take offense at it.

said that she never refused her hand to anyone, as she did not believe it to be a great favor. This attack made me blush, because I saw clearly that she was alluding to the fact that my hands are not pretty; but recovering promptly, I retorted, laughing as well: "It is true that my hand cannot be a great pleasure to kiss; but the secret conversations that you have with the marquis, what do you call those? You must decide here, and either confess that you have a conquest, or swear off your witty attacks." This repartee deeply embarrassed the marquise. The count took the opportunity to throw in his own barbs, and said that, according to all appearances, Madame d'Arcire would not renounce her wit, and that no woman alive would rather be suspected of having a love affair, than be attacked for her lack of wit or beauty. Brésy, who saw that his beloved was beginning to become embarrassed, came to her rescue and told her that, in any case, if these conversations were in fact a favor, as he was willing to admit they were because he found them so pleasurable, then the favor was so innocent that, if she never did him a greater one, he would have no cause to brag about her kindness.

"You have such an attentive manner and a merit so superior to others, that indeed, madam is in the wrong not to have advanced further with you already," the count replied to him; "but with a bit of patience," he added proudly, "you will make such progress . . ." "Ah, Count!" I interrupted, "let us not mix bitterness with our teasing; we are never separated from one another; nothing can be suspect in our actions, let us not disturb the innocence of our pleasures; and to calm our spirits, let us dance on the grass like shepherds[30] to the sound of the oboes." The count, ashamed of having shown his jealousy and wanting to inspire some in turn, took my hand with a gallant air to go dancing, and everyone regained a cheerful composure.

I made Madame d'Arcire very happy; it is not that the count's resentment did not make her triumphant, but she is wise, she feared a quarrel between two honorable men who would have pushed the issue too far. We danced long and very well. The old duke performed wonders, and even caprioled[31] to convince me of his good health.

---

30. Allusion to the pastoral novelistic tradition of the early part of the century, the most popular example being Honoré d'Urfé's multivolume romance *L'Astrée* (1607–28).

31. The *capriola* is a challenging dance step performed by jumping in the air and beating one's feet together.

With the dancing finished, we sat in a circle; and as night was approaching, and it was precisely the hour when everything takes on an indeterminate form, when trees seem giants and men mere shadows, the duke said, pointing out a thick bush fifteen or twenty paces away: "Is it not true that if you were alone, that bush would seem a group of spirits to you?" "I admit that my eyes could be fooled that way," I replied; "but I believe I have proven my self-assurance enough not to be singled out on the subject of cowardice." "As for me," said Madame d'Arcire, "I admit that I am sometimes afraid, and that I would not like to find myself alone here." At that point Brésy whispered something in her ear. Selincourt noticed this; and I started a story as quickly as I could, to ward off any future remarks that could have gone too far. "I assure you," I said, "that I am skeptical of visions because I have never had any; but I would die a sudden death if I saw something of that sort, unless," I added, "the apparition was of the nature of the one seen by a man I know. He was not a person of great importance; he traveled on a small, white horse, which also carried his suitcase: his business required him to stay at the main inn of a small town.

The day on which he wished to leave, his horse was no longer to be found in the stable; they searched everywhere for it until its head was seen to appear in the window of the hayloft, accessible only by a ladder. The host began to laugh, despite the chagrin of my friend, who could not imagine why or how someone had stashed his steed so high up. He was finally given clarification on the situation: it was a familiar spirit often seen in the house, subject to obsession with certain horses. The appearance of this particular one had apparently pleased him, and since the fact that its master had on riding boots led him to understand that the master was going to separate him from his new passion, he found a means to put the horse in a safe place. You could even derive a little moral from this and say that, spirit or not, nothing is impossible for love."

"Ah, as for that, mademoiselle!" exclaimed the count, "your moral is a bit far-fetched, for love, all-powerful as it is, could never, without devilry, make a horse enter through the window of a hayloft. But," he added, "I beg your pardon. I interrupted you inopportunely; the adventure is amusing, even if it might not be true. Please finish it." "That will not be difficult for me," I continued. "The host assured the traveler that he had to remove his riding boots and take on the air of a person settled in that place. His advice was followed, and the same power that had led the horse up to the attic, brought it back down to the stable. Not a moment was lost; the horse was saddled and bridled, and its master set off, much at ease for having duped the spirit: but it was he himself who ended up the dupe, for the poor little white horse withered visibly over the next few days, and finally died on the road."

There you have, madam, the short narrative I gave, which, having nothing frightening in and of itself, is so authentic that it must not fail to persuade the incredulous. The duke said that he had heard about a château in the Touraine region, where there was a spirit who was called "Monsieur." No one had ever been able to see his face; but he had a mass of crimped, golden blond hair, and always wore an English tailcoat made of taffeta, black in color, which made a lot of noise. "Monsieur was a teaser," he added, "he would pull out the servants' chairs while they were sitting around the fire, and after having made someone fall, he would burst out in long gales of laughter and try to catch another one. He subjected neither the master nor the mistress to this sort of taunting; but he often walked with them and laughed wholeheartedly when someone said something amusing. At first, they thought that Monsieur was asking for prayers; they had prayers of every kind made on his behalf: Capuchins[32] were even brought in. Monsieur made himself visible to them, but did not say one word in response to their questions. Finally, it was believed that a pure soul might be able to make him break his silence: the lord of the château had a very charming and very beloved son who, being only seven years old, seemed perfect for their plan: he was accustomed to seeing Monsieur, and had no fear of him. They asked him, nevertheless, if he would be willing to sleep alone in a bedroom that Monsieur was accustomed to frequenting; that they would light candles for him, and give him candy. The child assured them that he could not be happier to oblige. Everything was executed according to the plan, but the outcome proved tragic. The next morning they found the lad quite run down, and with a high fever. All that they could pull out of him was that Monsieur

32. These were monks or nuns affiliated with Saint Francis who were often summoned to pray for souls in purgatory.

had entered the room; that he had started by extinguishing the candles with the draft from his taffeta coat. The child then wanted to continue his narration, but he was taken by a fit of dangerous convulsions, which prevented him from doing so. He died a few days later, and Monsieur, after this fine feat, no longer appeared at the château de Montison."[33]

No sooner had the duke finished his tragic story than everyone began to pity a father and mother who caused the death of their son because of an ill-conceived piety.

Madame d'Orselis also wanted to have her say, but because she had not stopped listening to Chanteuil, or speaking to him, I could not keep myself from laughing, or from telling her that she had a sort of mind like Caesar, and that to listen to a pleasing man, without losing out on what the others are saying, seemed to me even more impressive than dictating to four secretaries at once.[34] This was a pleasantry that I let slip unintentionally; for as you know, madam, the beautiful Orselis is very intimidating, as much for her wit as for the loudness of her voice: she blushed and acted flustered for a moment; but gentleness typically accompanies a budding passion: therefore, in contrast to her usual manner, she responded to me that she could not deny that, since the chevalier has a charming wit, she took pleasure in his conversation, but that for all that she was not forgetting the rest of the company: "and to show you that I speak the truth, this evening I will tell you of an adventure that has more or less cured me of my fear of ghosts; but for that it will be necessary that I start my story from further back," she added laughing, "and that I inform you of almost all my past. I may even be cruel enough to bore you with a long account[35] to punish you for attacking me." We assured her that she could have our attention as long as she pleased, without being able to cause us a moment of boredom. With these words, we got back in our carriages to return to the château de Selincourt.

Dinner was served as soon as we had arrived; and since we usually

33. This medieval fiefdom, located in the Touraine region, had passed into the hands of a bourgeois family, the Robins, in 1626.

34. This account of Caesar appears in Pliny the Elder's *Historia Naturalis* (book 7, chap. 25).

35. See note 6 in the translation, p. 25.

went to bed very late, we played a round of bassette[36] before hearing Madame d'Orselis's story. She began to speak as follows.

"You know my family and my face; that is a great relief to those who speak of their past: but what you are perhaps unaware of is that I have inspired passion in men since age eleven. It is true that the first who took it into his head to find me beautiful was a man so far beneath me that he never had the audacity to tell me of his feelings; but he compensated for this respectful silence with gestures so fanatical and extreme during four straight years, that my mother was forced to ban him from her household, although incidentally he was quite entertaining. He invited three men, whom he believed to be my lovers, to go and fight him in foreign countries to avoid the penalties attached to duels in France ever since the reign of Louis the Great.[37] There were two who did not wish to take their anger so far, with whom he fought twice, with indecisive results; in the end, he was like a madman, and we did well to banish him. Among a fairly large number of admirers who proposed marriage, there was one who was a man of good breeding, intelligence, valor, and distinction. This conquest flattered my vanity. Never was there a passion so ardent and so constant as his; but there was another man, young and handsome as Cupid, and very much in love as well. If the first had had the looks of the second, or if the latter had had the intelligence of the former, the matter would have been easily settled, my heart would have been taken; but because they each had a weakness, or because my hour to love had not yet come, I was content to delight my eyes with the one and my mind with the other. Many quite extraordinary incidents took place, caused by opposing lovers and by the attempts that my family made to secure my establishment, which were often poorly directed. But I will spare you these trifles to come to something more serious.

I was married at sixteen to Monsieur d'Orselis; you are aware both of his high birth and his wealth: but I do not believe that you have ever met him in person, because his primary residence was in the country: he had

36. A Venetian card game, illegal in many places because of its high monetary stakes.

37. Although duels had been illegal in France since Richelieu's ministry (1624–42), under the reign of Louis XIV the ban continued to be violated from time to time, particularly by military officers.

a good stature, nice legs, very white teeth, quite ugly brown hair, large deep-set eyes, a looming gaze, dark yellowy skin, a disagreeably shaped face and four grooves marked in his cheeks, as if someone had furrowed them intentionally: he had wit; but a profound sadness; a predisposition toward rage, which his rational side could not control: jealous beyond imagining, suspicious, inclined to believe the worst; but despite all that a very honorable man, generous and lavish. He had a wild passion for me, which persuaded him that no one could see me without adoring me. This idea made me the unhappiest person in the world. He was jealous of kings, shepherds, and all the ranks in between; never did I have a quarter of an hour's rest: he was always in the throes of passion or in the fury of jealousy, and I was forced to suffer expressions of tenderness from a man whom I did not love, or to hear reproaches that I had not earned. It would be too tiresome to tell you all that I endured during this sad marriage, but allow me to tell you of one episode.

The Chevalier de . . . , a colonel in the dragoons,[38] passed through the city where I was then living, with his regiment; he came to pay me his respects, as to someone from one of the best households:[39] I did not know him at all; he presented two of his captains who were handsome youths, polite and charming. Monsieur d'Orselis was present: he was gracious enough that day, he invited them to supper; the Chevalier de . . . declined, and I had never received a more harmless visit; but I was not destined to go to sleep without chagrin. Monsieur d'Orselis proposed that we go to the home of the governor's wife that evening; he was in such a good mood, that I did not want to contradict him. We were surprised by the profusion of food and drink there, and we were preparing to sit down to a round of cards when we heard a loud noise and saw a troop of masked figures enter, bizarrely dressed, but stylish, though different from those one typically sees; the masqueraders brought with them all the violinists of the city, and the oboists of the chevalier, who were excellent; that did not leave a bad impression. The identities of the characters

---

38. This was the title given to the chief commander of a cavalry or infantry unit charged with fighting on horseback and on foot.

39. When a military unit passed through a region, it was customary for the heads of the regiment to pay their respects to the highest-ranking families as a gesture of goodwill.

were beyond doubt, but what was cruel for me was the preference they showed me.

The governor's wife did not have the right physique for dancing: there were lots of other women; and their scorn was no less than the rage of Monsieur d'Orselis, when the chevalier asked me to dance the first courante.[40] I feared the repercussions of this honor; I danced while trembling, even though I am not naturally shy, and I went to ask Monsieur d'Orselis to dance in an extremely obliging manner. He told me, with a face totally altered, that his foot hurt, and he refused me on the spot. Shamefully I took one of the masqueraders and then made my way back to Monsieur d'Orselis's side. 'You are very indulgent, madam,' he said to me, 'to let your hand be clasped as tightly as it just was.' 'Me, sir?' I said to him, 'What clasping? You must be imagining things.' He shook his head and left to keep an eye on me from beside the fireplace. One of the young men who had come to visit me, seeing my husband farther off, came to make small talk appropriate to such an occasion in a silly puppetlike jargon. Surprised when I did not respond, he cried out that he was very unfortunate to have crossed the seas only to find an ingrate. This was more of his puppetlike jesting, but the words stung the ears of Monsieur d'Orselis. He believed that this man had indeed crossed the seas, as if he had seen it for himself, and as he approached me he said to me, 'Are you being harried, madam?' 'I do not know what you mean by that, sir,' I said to him. 'Women like me are not harried.' 'I could restore order here in any case,' he replied defiantly. 'Oh! This place is no good for me,' said the masquerader in an ironic tone, 'I shall be thrown out for sure!' He moved away from me as he said these words. My husband felt his mocking to the core, and I do not know how he avoided ending up like Don Quixote on this occasion.[41] There were other circumstances that I am omitting in order to tell you that when we got home, I was treated as if I had been caught in wrongdoing; and what ultimately confirmed his suspicions was

40. A lively court dance for two people set to a triple-meter air.

41. Reference to part 2 of the picaresque novel *Dom Quixote* (1605) by Miguel de Cervantes in which the novel's eponymous main character confuses fiction with reality at Master Pedro's puppet show and destroys the illusion on stage. Most French readers of the time interpreted Cervantes's hero as an arrogant braggart and clown.

the fact that the same men who had refused his invitation to supper had come to my door to ask whether I was there; and only went to the home of the governor's wife after being told that was where we had gone. I lived only two years with Monsieur d'Orselis, and I could have started the story of his jealousy from the day after our wedding until the day he fell mortally ill. I do not remember spending a single happy day with him: since I was always under suspicion yet innocent, the compliments people paid me were a liability to me when I realized they would be used as fodder for my unhappiness. His illness was short: he spoke only of me, as soon as he felt the approach of death. His only regret was to leave me: I was young; I loved no one. The spectacle of a dying man, disarmed of the fury that made him someone to be feared, cannot be shown with impunity to a person who does not have an unkind heart. After his death, I no longer saw him as the terrifying husband who had tormented me without cause and without moderation. I saw him as an unhappy man who, agitated by a violent passion, had been unable to resist another passion a hundred times more cruel, which nature had given him only to torment him. In short, ladies, I cried, and I was very sincerely grieved. The maidservants of my friends who came to see me during this gloomy ceremony, where rooms hung in black never seem dark enough unless someone breaks their neck in there; these women, I say, imprudent to the utmost degree, came to rejoice with me that I had lost my tyrant. It was with a strange astonishment that they saw me shed a torrent of tears: I must admit, however, that my grieving did not last long, and that it can be better labeled pity than sorrow. I was raised to have very strict notions regarding all that concerns reputations; the more I realized that I was young, the more my husband had been disagreeable, the more I believed it was necessary to take certain measures. I was in Paris at the time: in that place, one is often exposed to the temptation to see too many people; I feared I would not always have the strength to shut my door to the large number of people who came to call. I decided to go and spend the entire summer on one of my family's estates with only my servants. I read, I took walks, I wrote to my friends, in short, I was leading a pleasant existence that did not bore me, when several nights in a row I heard noises over my head that did not seem natural to me: there were knocking sounds at regular intervals; there were sounds of rapid running; there was, in short, everything that was needed to frighten someone more fearless than I, for I was very cowardly in those days. However, I kept up a bold front for a few days, and wanted to believe that the noises came from animals that were coming in through the windows of the bedrooms above mine: what astonished me was that when I had company from Paris, the noises stopped, and the nighttime commotion did not recommence until I found myself alone again. I was sometimes quite afraid; but for all that I did not dream of leaving, and this was apparently what the spirit was aiming for. One night, the most terrible night of my life, I heard at the door to my antechamber a racket so tremendous that I could have believed it was burglars, more so than spirits, if they had not given the signal beforehand by three dreadful knocks right over my head; my maidservants were asleep in the bedroom next to mine, I called one of them, who was dying of fear: fortunately I had some light, without which she would not have had the strength to get out of bed; I ordered her to summon all her courage, and to yell, 'Fire!' out the window to make my valets come: the first who got up was my coachman, who came under my windows, armed with a scythe used to trim the hedges. We never found out why he arrived equipped with an offensive weapon to come to the rescue of people he believed to be in a fire; whatever the case, I was a little reassured when I heard a man speak; the difficulty was to get him in: no one had the strength to go open the door of the vestibule; because we were only women in the center of the house: finally, my coachman thought of utilizing the gardener's ladder. He climbed up proudly, as if he had stormed a position. While he was on the ladder, the same noise came from behind the door of which I spoke earlier. 'Aha!' he said, 'you speak of fire, when it is burglars; no matter, let them come, they will meet their match!' This warlike mood was inspired in him by my lackeys, who, having dressed in haste, came to support him in this great campaign. They all entered through my windows; and the ghost, apparently wanting to show off for them, rattled the partition which separated my bedroom from another with a devilish sounding noise. This ruckus was followed by a profound calm, but it did not penetrate my soul, which was shaken by the most violent fright that ever was: trembling in my bed, I barely dared to pull my head from under the bedcover. One of my maidservants approached me, pitying me and assuring me that, for fear of frightening me, she had not wanted to tell me all that she had seen and heard; that the anniversary of Monsieur d'Orselis's death was approaching, that he was apparently asking for prayers to be said for him; that he was advancing closer and closer in his walks, that perhaps the next night he would come to speak to me in person, and a hundred other visions that would have made me laugh at another time, but which, since my imagination was already unhappily stricken, made an impact on me that resembled delirium. I ordered my servants to go and find an abbé, who was only one league away from my home; he was a family friend, and a friend of mine in particular: I hoped for great solace from his advice. He arrived a short time after; by then, the sun was out. 'Ah, my poor abbé!' I said to him, 'am I not extremely unfortunate! Ghost stories are dismissed as tall tales, yet I have been chosen to experience the truth of them.' My demeanor was so afflicted, and my tone so distraught, that I hoped at least for a bit of consolation: but the unforgiving abbé made fun of me; and approaching my ear, assured me that one of my maidservants undoubtedly had a lover in Paris whom she wanted to see again. I thought to refute this statement. I wanted to appear neither as someone with a wild imagination nor as a dupe: I believed I would be able to prove to him that the noises being made did not come from human forces, and I concluded that we had to send for Capuchins to come and have a vigil in my bedroom. In response, he told me that prayers were always good. I went down into another room so as not to be in the place where I was filled with such cruel apprehensions. I told the same woman who had yelled 'fire' that she should go and fetch the things to do my hair. She came back a moment later more dead than alive, and collapsing at my feet, she said to me: 'Ah, madam! I cannot take any more of it; I have just come from your bedroom, we had made your bed; everything was clean and neatly arranged; I go back up just a moment ago, I find your mattress, your featherbed, your bolster, rolled up and stuffed like big dead bodies in your covers; I find your dressing table all overturned, your mirror face down, with the looking glass against the floor.' 'Ah!' I cried sorrowfully upon learning of this circumstance, 'it must be quite true then that Monsieur d'Orselis does not wish for me to take care of my appearance anymore, and that he torments me still after his death through the effects of his jealousy!' The abbé could not prevent himself from smiling, but he went upstairs to witness the confusion: he saw that the picture was accurate. He was astonished by it, all the more so because the woman who had given that description to see it did not seem at all suspicious to him, and she assured him that no one had gone up since my room had been cleaned. Large black claw marks were found imprinted on my door; to sum up, things had gone quite far: and as the presence of all my servants was not sufficient to reassure me, the same woman who had warned me of the vision of Monsieur d'Orselis told me again that, most assuredly, I should not stay in a place where he would certainly come to speak to me. It was in vain that the abbé offered to keep watch in my bedroom and to withstand the approach of the ghost. My fear had reached its maximum point; I had my horses harnessed to my carriage, I left for Paris, bringing the abbé along with me, not being fully convinced that the spirit would not appear to me along the way. He ridiculed me a lot for that, and for a vow that I made to undertake a small pilgrimage on foot, in order to please the ghost of Monsieur d'Orselis to leave me in peace. As soon as I arrived in Paris, the abbé, who had stayed in the courtyard, came up to tell me that he had just seen the spirit, that it was a tall, good-looking lad who was wooing at my front door the woman whose advice I had followed. The time had still not come to make me listen to reason: I carried out my vow the next day at the expense of my feet. Since several people in whom I confided my experience had assured me that there were no supernatural forces involved, I began to defer to their arguments, and I agreed to return to that estate with two or three women and a man who was very firm in his nonbelief in ghosts. I did not bring along the woman against whom suspicions had been raised. Everything was calm, not the slightest noise, not the slightest cause for fear; thus reassured, I returned to Paris, I spoke to this woman as her mistress, convinced of her insolence. She denied everything with conviction; but as I have seen nothing since, and as natural causes were possible for everything that I had heard, I resolved to take it for granted that there is no such thing as ghosts, and that everything that is told about this subject is false."

"That is easy to say, madam," I told her when I saw that she had finished her narrative; "but either fear had really magnified things, or what you heard was truly extraordinary." "It could well have been that in effect my predisposed imagination could have slightly exaggerated to my ears the things that seemed so terrible to me," Madame d'Orselis replied; "but given that this woman slept so close to the door where the noise was made, that this door had such thick bolts, that the bars of the windows were near her bed, such that she could have used them as she wished, and that she was the only one to keep her composure, she could have done whatever she pleased, without anyone suspecting her." "What Madame d'Orselis says is true," said the count; "love makes people undertake many other such ventures, and fear, which is in its way a passion just as strong, does not leave reason the leisure to do its job; and it often happens that one becomes attached to the sentiments that fear inspires, just as to the more agreeable ones: but," he added, "Madame d'Orselis has told us nothing of what has happened since that gloomy year of mourning; for I cannot believe that her heart is making its first attempt at love here." "You fire at me as well, Count?" she responded. "Do you not believe that it is necessary to exercise hospitality in all areas? It is not sufficient to offer us refined meals, to be attentive to our pleasures, to go above and beyond everything that could be agreeable to us; it is also necessary to treat a poor guest gently through one's wit and feelings: I regard you at the present hour as a man who has much generosity in his soul, and not the least bit of compassion in his heart; but, I do not find myself in the mood to get upset today," she added laughing, "and I will admit to you that I found on my path a man who loved me madly, whom I loved in return; according to the rules, this union should never have ceased: but do not ask me any more about it; for my best efforts to remain philosophical would not prevent me from mixing explosions of anger with my narrative; and I am still sensitive enough that I am unable to hear without sorrow the names that this man deserves by the way he behaved to me, names which you would inevitably give to him."

The beautiful Orselis sighed upon finishing these words; and Chanteuil, feeling his heart touched by a sorrow which augmented his love, said that it would be unjust to cause pain to a woman who had just shared such a pleasant narrative, and who had set the example for the rest of the company to tell a part of their adventures. "As for me," I added, "I will do so whenever you wish, provided that first, we retire for the evening." Everyone consented to that: but I must tell you, madam, that during the whole supper Brésy was making a spectacle of his newfound passion. The marquise responded with spirited glances, which gave him high hopes; but as for me, whose heart was not involved, I easily figured out that her coquetry was no more than a means of winning back Selincourt: this man was making a thousand equivocal remarks to me, which I could have attributed to myself; but glances in Madame d'Arcire's direction escaped him from time to time, motivated by spite. This is not a sentiment that proclaims indifference. The following day he made me a formal declaration: I did not feel it was appropriate to take offense to it; but I told him very sincerely that I held him in too high esteem not to advise him to return to his duty; that I saw the true motivation behind his attentiveness toward me; that I believed that he had succeeded; that the marquise was neither indifferent nor unfaithful; that he should cease a charade that could only have a regrettable outcome. "For either your beloved will give more and more hope to the marquis, or she will make him your successor," I added. "If it is the first, that man's nature is known to you; he will not lose his hopes without having his vanity suffer on account of it; he will invent an amorous adventure, rather than seem to have been duped: and if it is the other, you will be lost, Count; for you are madly in love; and you would be all the more to be pitied because you would have no one to blame but yourself." "But would you find me truly worthy of compassion, if you wanted to console me?" he retorted, "and have I not proven myself worthy of such consolation?" I interrupted him at these words to point out to him that Madame d'Arcire was getting up to go to her rooms; that the marquis wanted to accompany her, and that she did not want him to. I tried to compel Selincourt to follow her; but he is proud, and we had not yet reached the end of our troubles. You will undoubtedly be surprised, madam, that the count suffered so patiently, in appearance, a declared rival in his own home: but he had absolutely no right to complain about Brésy; they had been friends for a long time; he had kept his attachment to the marquise a secret from him: one cannot be expected to guess it. The count, who had really pretended to love me only to further the plan I mentioned to you, and in order to give a sort of rivalry to Madame d'Arcire, which the calm nature of their love had removed from her, had no sooner received a taste of his own treatment when, spite mixing with pride, he preferred to continue to express love to me, rather than to play the role of the jealous lover in a place where he was doing such a fine job as host. A few days after the conversation

that I had with him, we spent the entire afternoon indoors because it was
not nice outside. We played bassette,[42] we danced. We were joined by a
group from a neighboring town, half city dwellers, half provincial gentry,
who did not fail to amuse us. After we had exhausted all the ordinary
pleasures, we threw ourselves into conversation: the country ladies, who
wanted to show us that they had fashionable books, did not fail to turn
the conversation to the latest fairy tales,[43] on which they pronounced
judgment in their manner. There was one young woman who assured us
that all those things were just frivolity, and that for her, serious readings
were her greatest delight. Our little group was far from uneducated: we
wanted to know to what use she put those serious books; but she spoke to
us with a pedantry so shocking and made such affected grimaces, and her
erudition was so full of confusion that after having had as much fun with
her silliness as she deserved, Madame d'Arcire admitted that she loved
fairy tales with a passion; that she even believed that the ability to read
them with pleasure was a sign of refined taste. "It is not that I do not accept other sorts of reading material," she added; "on the contrary, I only
consider[44] these as amusement: but it must be conceded that when these
sorts of works are executed with the order supplied by artistry; when the
passions in them are tender, and when imagination is displayed in a brilliant and refined manner; you must concede, I say, that the hours pass
like moments during this sweet pursuit, and that time would hardly pass
more quickly with a beloved lover."[45]

42. See note 36 in the translation, p. 41.

43. The wording of this phrase bears striking similarity to the title of the collection of
fairy tales that Murat had published the previous year: *Les Nouveaux Contes des Fées: Par
Madame de M*** (Paris: Claude Barbin, 1698), containing six fairy tales in prose and one
in verse.

44. Since the French verbs *conter* ("to tell") and *compter* ("to count" or "to consider")
were often confused in early modern orthography, the phrase could be translated alter-
natively as "I only tell these for amusement." Catherine Bédacier Durand, the likely anagram of Madame d'Arcire, was in fact a well-known *conteuse* whose first published fairy
tale is contained in her novel *La comtesse de Mortane* (The Countess de Mortane; 1699),
mentioned at the end of book 1.

45. A reference to the passage of time on "the island of happiness," a fictional atemporal
space depicted in the eponymous fairy tale by Marie-Catherine le Jumel de Barneville,

The count had a great desire to contradict her, and the marquis to applaud her; but, destined as I was to calm the storms, I interjected to say that I had known for a long time a fairy tale that had previously been recounted in a well-known, noble residence,[46] in a time when wit was more fashionable than at present; that there was sufficient artistry in this tale; that if they wished I would share it with the company, provided that they did not require me to follow my text exactly, and that I could add to it a few embellishments that I thought necessary. Everyone jumped at my proposition: we were hosting our provincial group for two days; it was a question of interrupting for a while the boredom they were causing us: I began to speak in these terms:[47]

"In one part of the world there lived a great lord, tired of the gossip and the scandals of the court: he had demonstrated his valor and his worthiness until a well-advanced age. The desire to see once more the four sons whom he had fathered with a wife truly loved, who had died shortly after the birth of the last child, made him return to the château where his forefathers had lived, before receiving the royal pension that would have compensated him for his services.[48] He found his children old enough for

---

Countess d'Aulnoy. This dysphoric fairy tale, interpolated into d'Aulnoy's novel *Histoire d'Hypolite, comte de Duglas* (Hypolitus, Earl of Douglas; 1690), was one of Murat's favorites.

46. Likely an allusion either to the Marquise de Lambert's Parisian salon or to d'Aulnoy's salon on the Rue Saint-Benoît, both of which Murat frequented during the 1690s. The latter salon had recently been shut down due to a scandal involving the murder in 1699 of Monsieur Ticquet, husband of one of its primary animators. For that incident, see Duggan, "The Ticquet Affair as Recounted in Madame Dunoyer's *Lettres historiques et galantes:* The defiant galante femme," 259–76.

47. Tensions between the Parisian and provincial nobility were well known in the late 1600s and in large part created a market for journals such as the *Mercure Galant,* which professed to neutralize inequalities by keeping the provincial gentry so up to date on "news" from Paris that they would in fact know more about the latest fashions and occurrences of interest than the Parisians themselves would know.

48. The father's obligation to leave his family lands in order to serve the king at court or

him to make arrangements for their futures: they were handsome; they were intelligent; but their sojourn in the countryside had given them a certain awkward and timid manner, of which he could imagine only one means to cure them. He made all four of them come into his bedroom: he told them that his income was not considerable enough to make them well-off; that he found much injustice in giving the oldest son a larger portion than the younger sons, because they were of the same blood; that he was going to give each of them a share of his fortune; have the necessary horses and servants prepared for each of them, appropriate to their conditions; and he ordered the eldest son to go and seek his fortune in Asia; the second, to go to Africa; the third, to America; and the fourth, to Europe; that his health was good enough to hope to see them all return richer and more honorable men than they already were: they would meet up again in seven years, and if Heaven granted him life, they would find everything in such good order that they would have cause to bless and cherish his memory.[49] The four sons assured such a good father of their respect and obedience; they left not long after and followed the orders that he had prescribed to them: their adventures remain unknown, but they did not fail to go back, at the end of seven years, to their father's château.

They found him in good health; it was heartfelt joy for these five people to see one other again after such a long absence: the father, whose name was Mondor, asked his eldest son, who was named Haraguan, to tell of his voyage and of the skill he had perfected.[50] The son confessed to

---

in the wars echoed the situation of many provincial nobles at the end of the seventeenth century who were similarly constrained to leave their family homes, and often their families, to be of service to Louis XIV. The father's decision to leave the court before procuring a pension, however, would have been highly unusual.

49. The father's refusal of the primogeniture system of inheritance and his insistence that his sons, despite their noble birth, learn trades to support themselves would have constituted a radical idea at the turn of the eighteenth century.

50. All of these names are likely parodical. Given that "Mondor" was the name of a Parisian street performer who amused the crowds on Pont Neuf during the first half of the seventeenth century, readers would have immediately associated this character with a band of jugglers. The name "Facinety" evokes *fasciner* ("to fascinate") and *facétie* ("a joke"). The name "Tirandor" derives from the verb *tirer* ("to shoot"), and the name "Artidas" comes from the words "art" and "artifice."

him with some embarrassment, that he had had as his closest friend in Asia a prominent necromancer, and that he had become very proficient in this art.

'That is to say,' Mondor retorted, 'that to call the thing by its true name: you are more or less a sorcerer. And you, my son,' he said to the second, 'have you acquainted yourself with a science less dark?' 'My lord,' answered Facinety, 'I have become the most excellent illusionist[51] in the universe.' 'A con artist,' added the father: 'let's not obscure the facts.' Then, turning toward the third, he said to him, 'It is your turn to speak, Tirandor.' 'As for me, my lord, I boast of shooting more accurately than any man in the world.' 'Admittedly,' said Mondor, 'this is a bit more honorable. And you?' he added, looking at the youngest. 'Ah, my lord!' he cried, throwing himself at his father's feet, 'I must beg you a thousand pardons. I have become an artisan, without any respect for my noble birth; but if the perfection of my craftsmanship diminishes my fault, surely you will grant me forgiveness.' The sad father turned away, as if deeply engrossed in deep thought; his facial expression totally changed; one could clearly see that he was beginning to regret having sent his sons on voyages; but because he had strength of character, he pulled himself together quickly; and looking at them with a more serene expression, he said: 'You have certainly chosen professions worthy of neither you nor me; but it is necessary to figure out how to make the best of the situation, and to try to make the application of these professions you chose, rectify what is unworthy about them: there is, in the neighboring forest,' he added, 'something that will show me whether you are in fact as skilled as you believe you are: in fact, a bird that makes its nest only every hundred years has come to build it this year in one of these trees: the nest is a mystery to everyone; no one has ever found it: if you bring me to it,' he said to his oldest son, 'then you have not wasted your time in Asia.'

At once, Haraguan made some circles with his magic wand, and going outside with Mondor, he led him straight to the foot of the tree where the nest was. 'This is not bad,' said the father, 'but Facinety, here you must make a demonstration of your skill; climb up on the branches and go to pull the egg from under the mother without her noticing it.' Faci-

---

51. The French term *escamoteur* refers to a person skilled at making things vanish.

nety, lighter than a falcon, flew rather than climbed; and stealing the egg without the mother's suspecting it, he held it in the air at the top of the tree as a symbol of his victory. 'That is not enough,' added the father; 'it is necessary, Tirandor, that you shoot an arrow so accurately as to break the egg without injuring your brother's hand.' Tirandor did not miss his target; the hope of the bird was destroyed, and the egg fell in a thousand pieces. 'Artidas,' continued Mondor, 'here you must prove the dexterity of your hands.' Artidas did not waste a minute restoring the beautiful egg so perfectly that even the most discerning eyes would never have been able to perceive its flaws. The father seemed content with the trials that his sons had just undergone of their skills: he brought them back to his home; and speaking to them with the authority appropriate to the head of a family, he said to them: 'You have chosen appalling professions; but it must also be conceded that you excel at them, and that they need to be displayed in a theater other than a country château.'

'The king has lost his only daughter,' [Mondor continued]; 'she was more beautiful than the sun, she was intelligent, she was desired by all the neighboring kings, but her heart did not seem to have a firm preference for anyone: one day while she was walking along the palace terrace, she glimpsed a flying dragon of such tremendous size that she wanted to take off running to escape from it and get to her rooms; but the dragon, who had good eyesight, and who despite his weight was incredibly agile, took her in his ghastly claws before precautions for her safety could have been taken. This was terrible news for her father the king! He sent troops in every direction; he had fleets equipped to search all the islands in the sea; all his efforts were useless. It is a year since the princess was lost and no one has been able to get any news of her: if you can,' Mondor added, speaking to Haraguan, 'uncover where she is by the power of your art; this service would infinitely add to those which I rendered to the state in my younger years; and I would see you gather the fruits of them with all the joy of a loving father.' Haraguan promised to accomplish this important task: the necessary servants and horses were prepared within a very few days. Mondor took his family to the court; he presented himself to the king, who received him as a brave and loyal subject whom he wanted to reward, and his four sons like young lords of great promise. 'Sire,' said Mondor to the king, 'your majesty has not dried his tears; the cause of them is only too familiar to me; I cannot see my king grieving without trying to find a remedy.' 'And what remedy?' replied the king, 'could you bring to my sorrow? I have spared no effort to recover my daughter; I have not succeeded, nothing can console me.' 'Therefore, I have not come to offer you vain words of sympathy,' replied Mondor; 'you will find in the eldest of my sons a subject capable of rendering a great service to his king; command only that a vessel be equipped, and I promise you the return of the princess within two months' time.' The sad king shrugged his shoulders and looked at Mondor with pity; but as the old man was not discouraged, it was believed that, being a very reasonable man, he might in fact be able to deliver what he was promising. So a ship was prepared: the family embarked upon it, and after a month of navigation, they discovered an island where Haraguan assured them the princess was; soon after, they were even able to perceive the monstrous dragon, who was sleeping on the seashore and the sad Isaline (this was the name of the princess) trapped in fifty coils of the dragon's tail, which was more than 300 ells[52] long: she seemed to be watching intently and with tenderness a young fisherman who was sailing around the island, and who seemed to have a pressing desire to come to shore; but she signaled to him that he should move away: she showed him the ship; she clasped her hands. The handsome fisherman, whose clothing was tasteful and fashionable, obeyed her orders reluctantly: the eyes of these two people revealed their feelings for one another only too well; but Mondor, not wanting to lose any time at all, made Facinety get into the rowboat, had the boat lowered into the water, and told him to go and disentangle the princess from the tail of the dragon while he was sleeping, and to carry her on board the ship. This order, which would have frightened anyone other than this skillful illusionist, found him eager and ready to display the effects of his art; he disembarked on the island and carried off the princess in so little time that the whole expedition lasted no longer than a streak of lightning; happy to bring on board such a beautiful prey, he placed her in the ship, although the young Isaline did not seem grateful

52. Although this unit of measurement could vary somewhat from one region to another, the Parisian ell was three feet, seven inches and 8 lines. The dragon's tale, spanning more than 300 ells, would thus have been more than 450 feet long.

for this service. The young fisherman, however, made such piercing cries that the dragon woke up and, flying right over the top of the ship, he frightened all of the crew members with his horrible face: this dragon had only one vulnerable spot, and this spot was so small that an arrow could hardly penetrate it; but Tirandor unleashed one so accurately that the monster was deprived of his life. It is true that his death nearly proved fatal to our voyagers; he fell head first upon the ship, and split it down the middle; this brought in water with such great abundance, that it was all Artidas could do to repair it quickly enough to avoid being submerged; but it is true that this was so skillfully executed, that no one could ever see where the dragon had passed through.

All these events took place in so little time that Isaline, shocked and confused, could not figure out with what sort of people she had ended up. Mondor introduced himself to her: he told her that it was with the permission of the king that she had received these services from his sons. The princess thanked them with a melancholic air; and passing along the upper deck, she turned her beautiful eyes toward the island as if grieved to leave it. No one doubted that the handsome fisherman played a role in her sorrow; however, the lovers seemed to be ill-matched; the four brothers could not understand the peculiarity of such a preference; they did not realize that nothing is too far-fetched when two people are in love.

Haraguan, proud of the depths of his knowledge, was the first who wanted to assert the value of the services he had rendered the princess; he asked for his reward in the tone of a man accustomed to making the nether regions tremble, and more appropriate for addressing demons than a beautiful princess; therefore, he was received with anger. Facinety went about it with a more subtle approach: he sought out indirect methods, he chose the moment that he believed the most favorable; but though he was listened to with more patience, it was with no less lack of romantic interest. Tirandor, accustomed to never missing his mark, believed that his mere appearance would win her over; but he learned the difference there is between shooting at a bull's-eye and capturing a proud heart already spoken for. As for Artidas, his hopes were no less high; but he made his declaration through mathematical proofs. Isaline laughed at it, but he was no more fortunate than his brothers. They arrived shortly thereafter at the court; the king was on the docks, from afar he caught sight of his daughter, who was standing on the upper deck to make herself seen: her sorrow did not diminish the perceptible joy of the king; no sooner was she next to him, than he held her in an embrace for an hour, without being able to say a word; everyone took part in the joy of such a good father. He did not separate himself from his dear daughter except to give thanks to Mondor and his sons for such an important service, and to offer them all that belonged to him as a sign of his gratitude. 'Sire,' said Mondor boldly, 'we are your subjects, but my family is illustrious and ancient: this would not be the first time that a great king had chosen a son-in-law from among the nobility of his kingdom;[53] choose one, Sire, from among my four sons; the zeal that they have shown for your Majesty is basically equal; their merit is as well, and my affection for one is no greater than for another.' The king was struck by the audacity of these words: but he was not in a position to offend him: 'I believed that the rewards shared between you and your children would be sufficient to prove my gratitude to you,' he replied, looking at Mondor with benevolence; 'but because you consent that only one should be happy, I will grant you what you wish: since my daughter is to be the prize, it will be necessary to consult her before choosing; for now, go rest and savor the joy of being the father of such children.'

A few days passed and the princess did not seem to want to make a decision; she was melancholy and withdrawn. The king, her father, was asking her how she had spent her yearlong stay with the dragon. 'Peacefully, my lord,' she responded; 'my only sorrow was being unable to see you; but I believed that in the end you would forget about me, and that you would find a charming woman who would bear you successors. Moreover, the dragon exerted no cruelty over me: I had a small cabin made of leaves and I myself would pick the flowers that composed my bed; it was never too cold on the island where I lived; I walked every evening along the edge of the sea; I slept peacefully at night, and I kept myself busy all day by dreaming.' 'But what daydream could have amused you so agree-

---

53. This medieval custom had been progressively abandoned with the strengthening and centralization of the monarchy during the 1500s and 1600s. At the end of the seventeenth century the marriages of potential heirs to the throne were almost exclusively arranged to secure political alliances with the royal families of neighboring countries.

ably?' interrupted the king. 'You had no hope of coming to the end of your misfortune, you were under the power of a horrible dragon, and you had no one for company.' Isaline blushed at these words and lowered her eyes; then, raising them to meet her father's face, she said to him: 'My lord, you know that hope is a gift of nature, that it was created to console us, and that it dies only when we do; the dragon only compelled me to accompany him for a few hours along the edge of the sea when he wanted to go to sleep, and I had the complacency not to refuse him; I watched someone fishing during that time, and those moments were not the most disagreeable of my life.' 'Ah, my daughter!' cried the king, who saw her blush extraordinarily at this point, 'what's this I hear? You spent a year without boredom on a deserted island! You were unfazed by the sight of a horrifying monster, and your sweetest moments were when you were watching someone fish! Miserable fisherman!' he added, 'how dearly I will make you pay for the pleasure of having eased the boredom of an inconsiderate princess!' The king sent his daughter back to her rooms: he had Mondor summoned, he made him repeat what he had seen of this fisherman, which Mondor had already only too faithfully recounted to him. It was like a bolt of lightning for this unlucky father: he did not doubt that his daughter had let her heart be captured by an unworthy love, and he resolved to force Isaline to choose a husband from among the four young lords. Meanwhile, the melancholy princess being unable to keep her sorrow and her passion locked away in her heart, confided in one of her maidservants of whom she was very fond. 'They are going to make a crime out of the feelings that prevented me from despairing,' she told her; 'this king, this father, would no longer have a daughter if the young Delsirio had not appeared before me with all his charms: and what great charms he has, my dear Cephise!'[54] she added, sobbing; 'what heart could have resisted him! He would stand out in the middle of the most flourishing court. Imagine the impression that he made upon my thoughts on an uninhabited island; but perhaps he has forgotten me! The fickle man will be deterred by the obstacles that separate us!' Cephise,

54. The use of the name "Cephise" may be an allusion to the confidante of Andromaque in Racine's famous tragedy by the same name or to that of the title character in the opera *Alceste* by Lully and Quinault.

who was very glad to divert the princess from her sorrows a bit, asked her to tell of her adventures; she did so in these terms.

'You know, my dear Cephise, how I was kidnapped by that tremendous dragon; I thought I would be devoured by him a moment after, and I had resigned myself to it when he set me down gently on an island that was very pleasant but completely deserted; it was still daylight when I arrived there: the winged serpent took flight again and left me alone; I had no other thoughts but of death. "What does it matter how I perish?" I was saying to myself. "It would still be better to serve as fodder for the monster than to prolong a miserable life exposed to hunger and to the harmful effects of the air." I walked along, replaying these awful thoughts in my mind when I noticed on the sea a small boat, simple but pretty, and a young man who was fishing. Adonis,[55] handsome Adonis, never had so many charms; he had long, jet-black hair, beautiful eyes, a pleasant mouth, exquisite teeth, and a perfect figure; he cast his line with such grace, it made one want to imitate him, and his good fortune assured that he did not cast it unsuccessfully: his clothing was made of a delicate yellow cloth, hemmed with lace. He noticed how I was gazing at him in my distress. The opulence of my clothing, more than my beauty, doubtlessly attracted his eyes to me. "Great princess," he said to me, "what fatal star has brought you to these shores?" I recounted my adventure to him in a few words: he appeared moved by it, he leapt easily ashore in a manner both chivalrous and skillful, and even more eager; he went to cut tree branches, he made them into a very tidy cabin, he took moss and grass, he made a small, very comfortable bed for me with them, he scattered a thousand flowers on it; he assured me that the dragon was only cruel to those from whom he believed to have received some offense, and he asked my permission to come to see me every day.[56] I granted him this favor willingly. The trade that he practiced gave me no contempt for him: what prince could have claimed to have more beauty, grace, and wit than he? The dragon did not reappear for the rest of the day. My handsome fisherman came back the next day to the door of my cabin to hear whether

55. Adonis; see note 5 in the translation, p. 23.
56. The décor of the princess's rustic cabin is typical of many other fairy tales published at this time.

I was awake: he entered respectfully, once I signaled to him that he could. "Did you sleep, adorable princess?" he asked me. "Did your eyes, eyes so dangerous that they could steal repose from all mortals, taste the charms of slumber?" "Yes, Delsirio," I said to him. "I slept, and I believe that even if I had not, I would be obliged to tell you that I had after the care that you took to make me such a comfortable and pleasant bed." He sighed and made no answer; but he went a few paces from my cabin and took from the hands of a young fisherman a large, beautifully made, wicker basket: he opened it in my presence, in it I saw linens of surprising elegance, and some simple and refined clothes, more suitable to my current state than those I was then wearing, and a toiletry set with everything necessary for a woman. The trouble he had taken seemed to me deserving of reward. I asked him to go off for a short walk; I undressed myself during that time, I put on one of the dresses that he had brought me; and calling him back shortly thereafter, I took all of my jewels and I presented them to him in an appreciative manner. He took a few steps back. At first I thought that it was in astonishment; but a more noble feeling caused him to make this gesture; he was offended by what would have sent another man into an ecstasy of joy. What can I say, my dear Cephise? He vanquished me with generosity and I gave him in return a portrait of me that I was wearing on my arm:[57] he received it as if it were that of Venus. His delight was intense; but his noble air never left him, and everything about him was gracious. On that first day, I believed I was touched only out of gratitude; but I learned soon after that Cupid always hits his mark; that there is not a desert impenetrable to his arrows, and that difference in rank is no more than a weak obstacle when one is truly in love. Finally, I allowed him to speak to me as a passionate lover: I responded to him in almost the same manner. Every day he brought me small, rustic meals, but elegant and well prepared: we would eat them together. The dragon would often come to his island and did not seem bothered by our union; sometimes he would pick me up gently with one of his claws to take me with him to the edge of the sea: he would sleep

---

57. In this period men and women often commissioned miniature portraits of themselves and then exchanged these portraits with their lovers as signs of amorous preference, thus denoting a new level of intimacy in a relationship.

peacefully there. At those moments, Delsirio would jump into his boat and would sing tender airs to amuse me, for he has an admirable voice. This life seemed so pleasant and peaceful to me that, far from thinking of my return, I had no other goal than to establish myself on that island. Delsirio's social status was the only obstacle to this; but in the end, trying to rid myself of my prejudices, I concluded that I could indeed give my hand to the one to whom I had given my heart. As far as Delsirio was concerned, he had as much respect for me as he did love: he wanted to bring me around to his intentions gradually; but one day when he saw me more affectionate than usual, and when my eyes announced to him his total victory, he managed to take advantage of those moments so well that, unable to resist him any longer, and tired of fighting with myself, I held out my hand to him: and clasping it passionately, I said to him: "Delsirio, you love me; you know only too well how much I love you: no one will ever find me on this solitary island; the gods alone will be witnesses to our union, and I need not fear to be reproached by them, for they themselves have never disdained the mortal women whom they found beautiful. And after all," I added, "what do I care about how men will judge me when they learn of my choice? In all of the universe, I want only you." Delsirio, beside himself with love and with joy, fell on his knees before me and did everything typical of a man overcome by supreme happiness. We called upon Neptune, Thetis, and all the gods and goddesses of the sea to witness the vows that we were about to make to one another: we turned our eyes toward the gods who live on shining Olympus, and we had reason to believe that we were heard by them, because during the most beautiful evening in the world we heard a clap of thunder to our right, and we saw the sea become somewhat agitated, although it had been very calm before. That is how, my dear Cephise, we celebrated our nuptials. We could not doubt that the gods of love were present; for since that happy day, our bond to one another seemed stronger to us, although lighter, and each hour was marked by some new proof of passion until the fatal moment of our separation. Alas! The unfortunate Delsirio wanted to climb aboard the ship on which I was taken away: as soon as he noticed it, he did not doubt for a moment that cruel overzealousness was responsible for its appearance. But what could he have done alone and without weapons? I die of grief when I think of the sad life he leads at present, yet I fear even more that he enjoys a peace of mind fatal to my love. Marvel, Cephise, marvel at the degree to which I am obsessed with this love,' the princess added, 'for I have omitted the only circumstance that could justify my conduct, since my misfortune has led me to a place where I am subjected to the disapproval of men. On the day after our wedding, he informed me that he was the son of a king; that predictions difficult to understand, but terrifying, had obliged the king, his father, to send him away and to make him take on the clothing and the activities of a fisherman; that he had news from time to time from his father the king and enough money to live happily; that he had only one more month to remain in this state, after which he could return to his homeland; but because a peaceful life pleased me as much as it did him, he had decided never to return.'[58] 'Well then, madam,' said Cephise, after the princess had finished speaking, 'can you doubt that your delightful husband, after returning to his father's kingdom, will not come here next to ask our monarch for a possession that so rightfully belongs to him?' Isaline indeed hoped for it, but fear did not fail to find a place in her soul: she did not have long to struggle with this unhappy passion. The very next day, they had news that a young prince handsome as the sun, son of King Papindara, had arrived at the court to resolve a great mystery: it was the charming Delsirio. He requested a secret audience with the king: he told him of his high birth, his love, and his marriage to Isaline: everyone believed and marveled at his story. The king, who was a very good father, thought he would die of joy from it, and Mondor, who had high aspirations, was ready to die of grief. Haraguan found consolation because he was lavishly rewarded, and he was given one of the country homes of the king, Isaline's father, in which to practice his black magic. Facinety hoped to make as many women disappear as he could, even from the arms of their jealous lovers. Tirandor, preferring war and hunting to love, did not even bother to complain: and Artidas took his

58. The fact that the fisherman withholds his noble identity from Isaline until after the wedding takes place distinguishes this fairy tale from those of other late seventeenth-century French aristocrats in which the revelation of noble birth serves as a marital prerequisite. Murat's tale thus anticipates the socially equalizing role that marriage would play in eighteenth-century French fairy-tale production whereby such an extreme misalliance would be increasingly acceptable.

misfortune so well, that he even invented games and machines capable of surprising even the most ingenious people for the princess's wedding celebration, which they wanted to celebrate a second time with opulence; it was this same Artidas who invented double-bottomed boxes in which to put portraits:[59] he presented one to Isaline and told her that he could think of no better way to take revenge on Delsirio than to have him see this box containing a portrait of someone other than himself. The three youngest sons received rewards from the king capable of compensating them for any other loss besides that of the princess. Mondor also had good reason to be satisfied; and I hope, my ladies, that you are likewise with me after such a long tale, into which I have added enough material of my own invention to be unsure of my success."

When I had finished my tale, everyone rushed to give me praises, which I doubtlessly did not deserve, and they wanted to know what I had added to it. "First," I responded, "I told it according to my own style; I removed from it a simplicity that made it very short. The whole adventure of Isaline and Delsirio, their names and those of the rest of the characters, all of that is by me, and I do not feel that I am bragging too much by admitting it: the supernatural elements that are seen in other tales of this type are not present here; but also this tale is considerably shorter than those: I wanted to eliminate the fairies to see whether I could make my lovers happy without the aid of those good women, who correspond to gods coming out of machines, so condemned by the ancients."[60]

The count smiled when I finished these words: "I assure you," he said to me, "that you have put your erudition to a marvelous use, and that you do not read in vain."[61] "Do not make fun of me," I shot back at him; "I

---

59. A popular seventeenth-century trinket that allowed its owner to keep the object of his or her affection secret by hiding the beloved's portrait beneath another. See note 57 in the translation, p. 60.

60. The objection to using supernatural interventions to resolve plot complications was denounced as far back as Aristotle (*Poetics*, 1454a–b) and Horace (*Ars poetica*, 191–92); this would be linked to the seventeenth-century insistence upon verisimilitude.

61. As in the frame narrative of d'Aulnoy's recent collection of fairy tales *Contes nouveaux ou les fées à la mode* (New Tales or Fashionable Fairies; 1698), the fairy tale that Murat's narrator has just recounted exemplifies "literary orality": rather than being recounted purely from memory, it is read aloud with considerable embellishments.

am perhaps as formidable by my own ideas as by this erudition you reproach me for, and I could take revenge on you for your mockery." Selincourt asked me to forgive him: the conversation turned to more general
topics. This same countrywoman who had so criticized fairy tales praised
me for not having put fairies in the tale about the dragon: this did not
make me any more self-satisfied. The marquis said that it was a notewor-
thy thing that people with the brightest and most solid minds, who cen-
sure every frivolous pleasure, cannot stop themselves from reading stories
of this type, once they lay eyes on them. "This is doubtlessly the result,"
said Madame d'Arcire, "of the supernatural elements that one finds in
them, which are often far more agreeable than reality." "In my opinion,"
said Madame d'Orselis, "I think that the imagination that shines in every
aspect of these sorts of stories delights the reader's thoughts, and that
even the stern-hearted are cheered up when reading them, so to speak."
"I have a different opinion about them," I added, "and I am persuaded
that it is the truth one teases out of them, covered with an agreeable veil,
that pleases rational people: the truth is always appealing, but when it is
presented naked and without ornament, it has an element of harshness
to it; and if the count will permit me, I will remind you of a person from
antiquity who, having some unpleasant but necessary truths to convey
to a famous republic, had the whole population assembled in order to
announce to them, in a dour fashion, things which were somber in and
of themselves. He made everyone in his audience either yawn or flee:
and it was only upon making use of a fable, the appearance of which
contained nothing fatal, even though it communicated the same thing,
that he was able to bring back the audience members who had fled, and
even made his audience greater than before."[62] "What Mademoiselle de
Busansai[63] says is true," said the marquis; "but it should also be admitted,
however, that we have a natural affinity for the supernatural. As proof
of what I am saying, consider that there is no one who does not enjoy

---

62. The Republic in question is most likely Rome, where Menenius Agrippa, consul in
508 BC, calmed a group of insurgent plebeians by recounting a fable about an argument
between the stomach and the other body parts (anecdote taken from Titus Livy, *Ab Urbe
Condita* [*History of Rome*], book 2, chap. 32).

63. This is the only moment in the text in which the female narrator is named.

listening to ghost stories, even when they do not believe in ghosts; and I, myself," he added with a mocking tone, "I confess I amuse myself with them somewhat more than anyone else, even though I believe in them somewhat less." Our countrywoman maintained that, without denying the immortality of the soul,[64] one could not remain absolutely incredulous over these sorts of things. The men and the women of her group sought to defend her position with arguments in which they got quite muddled: next, they moved on to examples. They cited to us a thousand incidents that had occurred in their châteaux, which seemed absurd to us, and to which we attributed the causes either to the dilapidated state of their homes or to the feebleness of their minds. The Duke de . . . had kept a profound silence during this tumultuous conversation, but finally stirring, he said: "My ladies, I am no more of an idiot than the next man; I cannot be easily persuaded of the silly nonsense that people utter about souls in torment; but when I see people of solid minds telling me that they have seen such things, I find that it would be insulting to them and ridiculous of me to treat them as delusional.

Everyone knows Mademoiselle de C . . . ," he added. "It is known that she is neither small-minded nor lacking in courage: nonetheless, she herself told me that one of her friends, leaving for the army (you understand, ladies, what women mean by 'friend'); this friend then, taking leave of her, assured her that if he were to lose his life during this campaign, he would appear to her in white if heaven granted him mercy, or in a fire if he were condemned. Mademoiselle de C . . . consented to this idea; several months passed, during which time she received news from him too frequently to fear anything fatal; but one day when she was reading, leaning on a small table, she saw a dismembered hand place a golden box on that same table: the hand disappeared. Trembling, Mlle de C . . . reached for the fatal box: she opened it, and found that it contained a heart, like one out of a cadaver that has just been opened. The horror of such a sight

64. Allusion to Descartes, who addresses the separation of the body and the soul in his 1641 *Meditationes de prima philosophia* (Meditations on First Philosophy), particularly in the sixth meditation. This treatise would become the basis of an extended debate over ghosts in the *Mercure Galant* between 1692 and 1698. Defenders of belief in ghosts sometimes used this argument, which could also be linked to the belief in the punishment of souls in purgatory. See also the Introduction by Allison Stedman (hereafter Introduction).

made her look away: at that moment, she heard a noise in the fireplace, as if a fire were blazing there; and she saw a dark, bluish fire descend, consuming a body which she recognized all too well as belonging to her unfortunate friend; grief and apprehension caused her to faint. One of her maidservants, who was at the other end of her bedroom and who had seen nothing, rushed to her aid and revived her a few moments later. She ordered countless prayers, even though she believed they would be useless judging from the nature of the apparition. She found out that same day that the man in question had received a mortal blow during a siege, from which he had died not many days later; and the box with the heart in it, which was left with her, cannot leave any doubt as to the authenticity of this adventure."

The marquis began to laugh inconsiderately. "Why, Duke!" he cried, "Are these the sorts of things you wish one to believe? Do you not see that an imagination struck by the promise of this friend would have been capable of presenting her with even more frightening apparitions; and that in order to avoid being called crazy, she had the heart of one of those animals whose noble parts resemble ours put in a box to give more credibility to her story?" Everyone laughed at the marquis's joke; and without wanting to look more deeply into the matter, we chatted idly until supper about a variety of subjects.

The marquise was more animated that evening than she had been up to that point; she was as pleasant to me as one could be. Never had Brésy believed to have advanced so far, and never had the count felt a greater need to involve me in his interests in order to distract him from his sorrows; but no matter how much he tried to restrain himself, jealous spite was evident in his eyes, and I feared on several occasions that, despite the ancient right of hospitality, he would find the slightest excuse for quarreling with the marquis. The country group left us the following day after dinner: the count could hardly contain himself any longer; Brésy was no less proud: Madame d'Arcire feared what would happen next, but she did nothing to bring order to the situation because her beauty was being more and more celebrated as the tension increased.

To sum up, madam, it would be shocking that two honorable men could have been jealous of one another with impunity, but the count was in his own home, the marquis was his guest; both were obliged to show consideration, both were vainglorious, both presumed their merit to be infinitely above that of the other; one being armed with a spite that obliged him not to accept being offended, and the other flattered by a hope that did not allow him to withdraw, they only allowed themselves the freedom to lob some mocking remarks at one another; but it did not get to the point of an actual quarrel. It is true that the count, having made a great effort to control himself, soon resumed the tactic of pretending to be in love with me: that evening, he proposed that we should go to have supper the following day in one of those pretty houses whose owners are overjoyed to let people visit when they are not there: the home in question, which is in . . . has not a single tree that is not surrounded by flowers; the grass plots there have walkways composed of sand of ten different colors; the fountains are ornamented only with grass; but the manner in which they are maintained makes them preferable to marble; the gardens are full of splashing fountains that never stop running; the view from a terrace that borders the garden is a painting in which all points of view are worthy of admiration. In summary, Monsieur de R . . . is a man of taste in all things, and he is no less deserving of praise for the land he chose as for the foreign ornaments he brought to embellish his pretty home; thus, it was this place that we chose for our stroll. We thought to go there by water because this house is situated right on the banks of the Seine. The oboists were in a boat that followed our own: both were gallantly decorated. The weather was marvelous, everything seemed to radiate joy; Chanteuil and the lovely Orselis let a charming joy shine in their eyes, Brésy had a lot of love in his, the marquise wanted to respond to it, the Duke de . . . put to use all the gallant formulas of his time to seduce my heart, and the count did a marvelous job of playing the role of the declared lover at my side. You know, madam, that there is a sweetness in being preferred: I was thus greatly predisposed to being joyful, and the conversation, which was general at first, was assuredly not bad; but imperceptibly, the harmony of the oboes and the sound of the current inspired in us a short dreamy silence; and a moment later, after Madame d'Orselis had said something to Chanteuil in a soft voice, the marquis felt himself justified in speaking in the same tone to Madame d'Arcire. Selincourt did the same with me, and the duke, who was in love only to fit in with the company, went to sit at the other end of the boat when he saw me occupied with his nephew: I was not so occupied that I did not see that the marquise kept glancing unintentionally at us, which proved that she was not paying much attention to whatever Brésy was telling her. I saw that Brésy noticed it as well, and that he looked at her spitefully for it. "In truth," I said to the count, "you are causing a terrible disorder among our little society: you are in love with the marquise, I am sure of it; her heart is receptive only to you. What pleasure can you possibly take from hiding your true feelings in order to convince me of a passion that I find wrongly kindled, in order to torment a charming woman who is in love with you? If you had not taken it into your head to play the role of the flirt at an inappropriate time," I added, laughing, "you would now be peacefully enjoying the pleasures of a tranquil love affair, and the marquis, who upon arriving here was ignorant of our various interests, and who believed me to be linked to you, might possibly have turned in my direction, had he believed me to be without a suitor: I might possibly have listened to him favorably: you would be happy at present. Instead, the situation has become so confused that we should all be fearing a catastrophe, and the best that can come out of it is that I will end up alone." The tone in which I finished this speech did not allow Selincourt to respond to me very seriously; therefore, after having admitted that eternal calm in amorous adventures caused him a lot of boredom, and that regardless of the price that he would have to pay, he rather liked a little bit of agitation, he assured me that he found me very attractive; but that the original motive that he had had in attaching himself to me had been to make the marquise a little jealous; and that subsequently, the manner in which she had received the marquis had made him determined, either to cut her to the quick to make her return to him, or to try to love me sincerely in order to compensate for having an unfaithful beloved. "You must find me very philosophical," I answered him, still laughing, "to tell me so nonchalantly of the motivations behind your affection for me. If I were an ordinary woman, I would become your irreconcilable enemy, nothing is more difficult to pardon than an attack on one's beauty; but I forgive you for your little ruses of war, and I will not count myself any less among your friends," I added, extending my hand to him. The count, who was gallant, kissed the hand that I was holding out to him with an air of gratitude, and accompanied this action with some rather gentle words. By chance, I caught a glimpse of Madame d'Arcire at that moment; I saw in her eyes a mix of jealousy, anger and pain, and I noticed that she lowered a large headdress that she was wearing on her head, and that she leaned against the boat. We arrived shortly thereafter.

It was quite hot out: we spent several hours in a large sitting room that looked out over the river. Madame d'Arcire still kept her headdress down, on the pretext that she had a very bad headache: the marquis played the role of the doting lover at her side. The count went up to them in order to express his sympathies to her; but she received him with the sort of pride that can always be interpreted as a favor from a polite woman: however, she did force herself to talk a little, everyone took part in the conversation, but as the majority of people were feeling awkward, I took it upon myself to remind the company that, following the example of Madame d'Orselis, we were all supposed to give a brief history of our life, or at least recount a few episodes from it. Everyone wanted me to begin; I said that I was not in the mood to speak for very long; but I proposed we draw straws: the Chevalier de Chanteuil drew the short one, and he began to speak as follows.

"I will not bore you, ladies, with all that has happened to me during my lifetime; that would be either sad or dull: I have often been unhappy, often abandoned; and although I have been accused of infidelity, I have good reason to appeal this judgment, and you will see a proof of this in a story, which without being filled with important events, is nonetheless among the most peculiar.

Four years ago, after having seen a lady for a long time as a friend, I took it upon myself to love her as a beloved. This woman, whom I will refer to as Madame d'Arsilly, is very likable, both for her appearance and her intelligence; I began to find charms in her that I did not find in others; she seemed to me sweet and even-tempered, the liveliness of her imagination gave her a penchant for jealousy: it was to this passion that I owed my happiness; in vain did I change my style and my behavior in her presence: she could only view me as a friend. A pretty young woman who often visited her home, and whom I took it upon myself to praise, made her decide to make a little more effort in my favor in order not to lose me. I became happy, ladies, and I can say so without indiscretion because my

happiness consisted only of the tender feelings she had for me, but happy
in the most charming way in the world. Madame d'Arsilly was affectionate, attentive, faithful, and wary as much as was necessary; she lacked
none of the qualities that make one's happiness perfect. For three months
I had been the most fortunate of men, and I could not believe that it had
been more than three days when I had to leave for a military campaign.
Unhappy duty! Inopportune glory! How cruel the approach of this separation was to us! 'I am going to leave,' I said one day to Madame d'Arsilly.
'In this life, one cannot enjoy lasting pleasure! I am going to leave, and
you will be left exposed to the dangers and the unhappiness of absence;
it is sweet to me to think that you will share the latter with me,' I added.
'Yes, madam, I am cruel enough to wish that you will suffer; but what
will assure me that you will not abandon a lover who can only be at your
feet for a part of the year? Who during six months can make no other
vows to you than those one makes to God? Might you not make some
fatal choice . . . ?' 'Ah!' Madame d'Arsilly replied to me. 'Enough of this
offensive speech; I have proven my love for you too well for words to cost
me any effort.' After that, she told me everything that can bring calm to
a heart, and I left even more in love with her than I had been on the first
day."

    "You did well," interrupted Madame d'Orselis, "to spare us the rest of
that conversation; those of that type are always too short for the lovers'
taste and too long for the taste of the others who listen to it." The bitterness of this interruption annoyed the chevalier. "I will try," he said, "to
keep that in mind: the authority with which you speak to me does me
too much honor; however, madam, I should add that the interesting moments of the story are hardly more significant;[65] there are no kingdoms
overturned, no battles won or lost, no cities under siege. If those sorts
of events are important to you, I run the risk of boring you; but if the

---

65. This translation follows the 1734 and 1788 editions. The text of the 1699 edition contains a typographical error, which leaves open the possibility of an alternative translation:
"the interesting moments of the story are not about important wars." Both versions of the
sentence suggest the elevation of private "particular" history over public "official" history,
a genre that had served an important role in the memorialization and proliferation of the
absolutist political narrative.

singularity of feelings has some merit in your view, I will continue my narration, only too happy to occupy your attention for a moment."

The slightly mocking smile that accompanied these last words made me judge that there would soon be one of those quarrels between them that increase love when they are rare and that destroy it without fail when they happen too often. Chanteuil resumed his story as follows: "During the whole campaign tokens of reciprocal love were exchanged, and upon my return, I found my beloved more beautiful and more affectionate than upon my departure: never has anyone felt the pleasure of being reunited more acutely than we did. One of Madame d'Arsilly's maidservants let me into her home at an unusually late hour. No one expected to see me for another three or four days: I must admit that I was well received. After a conversation lasting three or four hours, I went off to dress a little more formally to make my official return visit. There were quite a few people at Madame d'Arsilly's home: I made a serious ceremonial speech to her which nearly made her lose her composure; she was lucky to be in the company of Madame de V . . . , whose brain full of witticisms furnished her with excuses for laughing. A part of the winter passed in the most perfect delights; I saw the woman I loved every day: one of her friends often had us over to her home; we had the pleasure of having light suppers in good company where constraint was banished.[66] But nothing is stable under the sun; I had been in love with Madame de Vaubry; Madame d'Arsilly was aware of that. The latter lady knew that I had supped with the former: it was enough to accuse me of getting back together with her. The fact that I wanted to keep it a secret from her irritated her; she persecuted me for a month with ill-founded accusations. I was no longer anything more than a friend of Madame de Vaubry; but I did not want to sacrifice her to the whims of a rival's unfounded jealousy: I resolved to see her from time to time, and to hide it from her as if it were an illicit action.

But Madame d'Arsilly is not among those easily deceived. She entrusted one of her maidservants with corrupting one of my servants in order to find out my comings and goings; he was only too willing to oblige. One day when we were supposed to have supper at the home of

66. See note 14 in the translation, p. 28.

this friend about whom I have told you, someone came to inform Madame d'Arsilly that I had supped the night before with her rival; I had not yet arrived: a thunderbolt does not come close to the effect of this all too accurate report: she confided it to her friend. I was condemned without chance for appeal, and my beloved received me very coldly; I went up to her, I took advantage of the freedom I had in this place to whisper to her; she responded to me in two or three ambiguous monosyllables, which women use when they are angry; I was in despair, the supper dragged on quite painfully. Since Madame d'Arsilly was generally the life of the party, we could not enjoy ourselves because she was in such a bitter mood the whole evening; I barely obtained permission to bring her home. She did, however, give me permission to come in; it was then that she told me everything that rage makes one say when it takes over one's emotions. Madame de Vaubry was treated as a mortally hated competitor. I assured her of my innocence; I admitted to her that I had seen this woman, but that it had been in accordance with the actions of an honorable gentleman who should never stop seeing a woman who had once been his mistress when he had no good reason for doing so: finally, I took such good advantage of a fortunate moment, in which a tender heart softens after a violent lovers' quarrel, that I made my peace with inexplicable charm. We never had any more quarrels about Madame de Vaubry because that lady left Paris. I loved Madame d'Arsilly as much as it is possible to love someone; her love for me was no less: our days passed in a peace and a harmony that took nothing away from our passion, for it is necessary to say in her favor that, in addition to a lot of wit, she has even more imagination, which makes her one of the most amusing people in the world when she is around people she likes.

If we had some small spats, these served only to further increase our ardor. Up to now, ladies, you have only seen flowers; presently I will show you the thorns: I thought I noticed, toward the end of the winter, a bit of coolness in the behavior of the charming d'Arsilly; she daydreamed a lot, she kept looking at her clocks to see what time it was: when I tried to complain about it, she gave me poor excuses; always distracted or sorrowful, she found the secret of making me yawn in her presence: then her self-esteem suffered. She accused me incessantly of being bored with her, which annoyed me in turn: I left her house irritated, and when I had had the time to reflect upon what I would be losing if she no longer loved me, rage took over my heart; I acted in ways that only passion can excuse.

One day, the cruelest day of my life, I arrived at her home: a slight headache confined her to her bed; she received me with an air that chilled me to the bone. I went to her side, I took one of her hands: 'What is it, madam?' I said to her, 'what have I done? What have I even thought that could have displeased you? Are you tired of my passion? Is there another fortunate enough to take my place? Answer me, madam, answer me; your silence makes me envision all sorts of terrible things: the most horrible would be without a doubt to have a preferred rival; but who could this rival be? Where could he be hiding? Are the eyes of a jealous lover not perceptive enough?' I added. 'Ah, madam! You are killing me!' 'What do you want me to say to you?' she asked me, looking at me with large distracted eyes that brought fury and unrest into the depths of my soul. 'What would I like you to say to me?' I retorted; 'have I not explained my concerns to you fully enough?' 'All that is left,' she replied, 'is for you to make your decision: I was in love with you, I thought I would love you forever; however, this is no longer possible for me.' 'Ah, madam!' I cried out to her with a horrific tightening in my heart. 'Is it really you who speak to me in this manner? Who would ever have thought it? To what do I owe such a cruel disgrace?' I was watching her while speaking thus, with a look that would have caused even a tiger to take pity. She even had the satisfaction of drawing some tears from my eyes; but her own eyes stayed dry: harshness and indifference were evident in all of her actions: hardly moved by my despair, which was bursting out with violence, she held out her hand to me, and said to me in a manner that would have made anyone die of rage: 'Now don't be so upset, chevalier.' 'Oh, leave me be, madam!' I replied, pushing her hand away; 'I do not want your pity, only tell me what has caused your change of heart.'

'You know,' she said to me, 'that you gave me a horrible jealousy over Madame de Vaubry; that passion animates some women; with me, it cures me sooner or later.' What joy I felt at this deceitful speech! In my opinion, I had enough evidence to prove my fidelity; but soon, calling upon what was left of my reason, I responded to her, 'No, madam. You cannot trick me; you knew of the feelings that I have for Madame de Vaubry: a happy time has passed between us since that storm when you were sure of my heart, and I was also sure of yours,' I added. 'Cruel one! You only add lies to your treachery!' At these words, I insisted on leaving: I listened in vain to see whether she would call me back; I came back to shower her once again with reproaches, and her coldness, which was extreme, made me act like a madman.

As soon as I got back to my house, I gave way to my various emotions: I fulminated, I thundered; but I still loved her with an unparalleled ardor: and my weakness was so great that I went back the very next day to see my faithless one. I found her beautiful and elegantly dressed; she received me without embarrassment and without fuss. 'Chevalier,' she said to me, 'you did well to come back; one must not cause a scene. If you had stopped your visits, that would have provoked gossip and my reputation would have suffered from it.' 'This is all you care about, while you are driving me to despair?' I cried. 'You have not chosen your chevalier carefully, madam,' I added. 'What do I care what people will say about you? I may be dead before this day is over.' After that, I threw myself at her feet; I did outrageously demeaning things. I asked her to deceive me out of compassion. 'I am unable to, Chevalier,' she said to me, 'my sincerity always takes precedence over my other feelings: try to console yourself, I feel no inclination whatsoever to give you any further solace.'"

"In truth, Chevalier," I interrupted, "Madame d'Arsilly was a madwoman and you were a perfect lover of whom she was very unworthy." "How so?" the beautiful Orselis interjected. "I feel one should follow one's preference. A love affair should be a source of pleasure; it is tyrannical to allow tedious constraint and subjugation to transform it into a source of dread." Madame d'Arcire did not say a word; the count and the marquis kept a profound silence; the duke had dozed off; and after Chanteuil had begged us to suspend our judgment until the end, he resumed his speech as follows.

"Several days passed, during which I rarely saw Madame d'Arsilly; but instead I carried my pain everywhere, I bored everyone I was with: the mere sight of a servant wearing Madame d'Arsilly's livery caused me to be seized by heart palpitations which would last for the rest of the day: it was a violent state, it was impossible for it to persist without some change. At that time an opera was playing which interested people of importance. I allowed myself to be driven there: I saw Madame d'Arsilly from afar in the audience, lively, gay, even coquettish. The Duke de . . . was behind her, who doubtlessly was not boring her. Jealousy and spite mixing together made me resolve to take revenge; and in order not to be outdone, I struck up a conversation with a pretty woman who was opposite my faithless one. She occasionally turned her eyes toward this new spectacle: for her, it was one that she was not expecting, and as ladies do not like to lose suitors, I noticed some vexation in her gazes.

The person with whom I was conversing did not have reason to find me very witty; whenever I would randomly pay her some sweet compliment, I would look at Madame d'Arsilly and her new lover in spite of myself. 'So there is the cause of her change of heart,' I would say to myself. 'I know whom to blame, I know whom to hate. Ah!' I continued, 'I owe my hatred only to the woman who has betrayed me.' You can easily judge, ladies, that a man who talks to himself in this manner cannot be having a very logical conversation, but she liked it better than nothing; perhaps she too had her reasons to appear pleasant. The following day I went to the theater. I found Madame d'Arsilly there; the Duke de . . . did not fail to show up: he had his box opened for him. There again, I found my beloved from the previous day and I counterattacked as best I could; however, that evening I had been invited to a supper that Madame d'Arsilly was also expected to attend at the home of a woman who was not aware of our breakup: I thought I noticed an affected joy in her speech and in her demeanor; she blushed each time I pronounced the name of this woman whom chance had made me encounter: she looked at me from time to time in a manner designed to make me confess my fault to her; but I remained in control of myself until after supper. Everyone sat around the fire as they wished. Madame d'Arsilly did not seem upset that I placed myself next to her: I told her things capable of stirring emotion in boulders; my eyes were full of tears; I noticed that hers were responding in kind. 'Chevalier,' she said to me, 'keep yourself for me; excuse my fickleness: it is true that I have an ill-fated passion in my heart; but I will come back to you one day: you are an honorable man, I hold you in high esteem, I have no more than a passing fancy for the man whom you rightly judge I prefer over you: once again, do not commit to another.'

She was so beautiful and so touching as she spoke to me; shame and remorse were so clearly painted on her face that, unable to throw myself at her feet, I lowered my head down to my knees to thank her for such a bizarre declaration, which the passion I felt for her made me receive favorably. 'Ah, madam,' I said to her, 'end it! Break ties that are unworthy of you. The Duke de . . . is pleasant enough: he has wit; but he has very odd morals and principles: one day you will regret that you preferred him to me, even for a moment.'

'You know that reason does not regulate love,' she interrupted. 'I have told myself more times than you could possibly tell me. But Chevalier, I am more in love than anyone has ever been; take pity on me.' At these words I could no longer control myself, and looking at her in an irritated manner, I said to her, 'Ruin yourself, madam, ruin yourself, I no longer want to be involved in this: you are a very flawed imitation of the Princesse de Clèves:[67] your crime is more complete and more outrageous and your remorse is not as real as hers. Enjoy with the Duke de . . . pleasures that you will have the time to regret. Let me free myself from your chains; do not come to me anymore with a poisonous demeanor, promising a reunion that can no longer be pleasing to me when your heart has been profaned by the image of a man like the Duke de . . . . Besides, you only want to win me back to serve your own self-image; you would want to make me a pawn in the triumph of my rival. Ah! Rather that . . . !' At these words, having seen her sigh and weep even more, I felt myself disarmed; I found her behavior as noble as it had seemed extraordinary to me, and I had the weakness, when I brought her home, to come in and to stay there until four o'clock in the morning, without receiving anything sweeter than the assurance of a return.[68]

You see, ladies, how crazy one is when one is in love: I left the home of the unfaithful d'Arsilly a happy man; I found in her the worthiness of a Heroine. I loved her more than ever. I went back the following day in the evening; but I found her cold, preoccupied; her responses were

---

67. The heroine of Lafayette's famous novel, *La Princesse de Clèves* (1678), avows to her husband that she desires to retire from court to avoid amorous temptations. The two women thus resemble one another only in the shocking sincerity of their declarations.

68. That is, than the assurance that she would come back to him eventually.

distracted; I quarreled with her with an intensity that would have made anyone tremble; she was not moved by it that day: full of her passion, and charmed by having seen her former lover more in love than ordinarily, all other objects seemed disdainful to her. My fury drove me to seek out my mistress at the opera; I found her, I followed her everywhere. Madame d'Arsilly was a witness to it, for she never missed a spectacle or a stroll in order to have the pleasure of seeing the Duke de . . . . Some days later, I received a note from her, which I retained by heart. It ran as follows:

So you want to leave me! And my consternation, instead of inspiring your pity has only provoked your anger! Are actions caused by a whim of destiny always unpardonable? Destiny has affected me only too strangely. I have been led to commit a kind of infidelity against you, but only with my eyes, while my heart still belonged to you. But you, Chevalier, you love Madame de . . . because you want to love her: you offend me deliberately, and I will perhaps be pained to find you truly committed to her, while I offer you a sincere and lasting reunion.

I responded to Madame d'Arsilly's letter in this manner:

These delicate distinctions, whose falsehood and artifice I recognize, should find in me nothing but a harsh critic, ready to send you back to your thoughtless and indiscreet lover; but, I love you: this word alone will justify my weakness; too happy to be reunited with you, I would certainly refrain from making reproaches that would only remind you of a rival who is loved too well, and this afternoon I will go and receive the return of a heart blackened with treason, with the same submissiveness as if I were the one at fault.

Admit, ladies, that you find me quite mad: I was, more than you can imagine; beside myself with joy, moved by gratitude, I ran, I flew to the feet of Madame d'Arsilly: she was more beautiful than love itself; the redness that her shame was causing her made me find her adorable: it was in those precious moments that I understood that one must pass through pain in order to arrive at pleasures.

We enjoyed a peacefulness that was troubled only by the strange stories recounted by the Duke de . . . regarding his short love affair with
Madame d'Arsilly; and through the relationship that formed between
him and the lady whom I had abandoned, they tormented both of us in
every way: I was so much in love that I was ready on several occasions to
fight for my beloved's honor; but some of our mutual friends put a stop
to our plans. I had never found Madame d'Arsilly so charming: for her
part, she attempted to erase impressions that she thought had remained
with me; but it was not my destiny to engage her affections permanently.
A few days before my departure for the army, I found her once again in
her chilly demeanor; I attributed it to the temperamental nature of her
sex: she once again had the sincerity to confess to me that it was a second revolt of her heart, which was feeling love once again for the Duke
de . . . . This time I felt more indignation and disgust than anger; I left
for the army more or less at peace, without taking the trouble to quarrel
with her: I went four months without writing to her, and I would have
pushed my indifference even further, if I had not learned that she had
had a violent illness; I felt obliged to pay her my sympathies on that account: I was wounded at the time: she in turn extended her condolences,
and upon my return, I have no idea how this happened, but we got back
together for a third time: I even gave her evidence of my commitment,
which would have touched any other woman: but in this final round,
since her love had gone up to a certain point, it could not longer maintain the same intensity and degenerated as on the other occasions. I do
not know if my passion was spent, or if my reason intervened; but I broke
up with her, without ceasing to be her friend, however, and I put myself
in a position to see myself with more self-respect in amorous servitude to
someone other than her."

The Chevalier de Chanteuil, upon finishing his narration, looked tenderly at Madame d'Orselis, in order to make amends for the somewhat
too harsh comment that he made to her when she had interrupted him.
"On my honor," exclaimed the count when he saw that Chanteuil was
no longer speaking, "Madame d'Arsilly is a very peculiar person! You
displayed patience of an unusual variety while you were courting her."
"Well," said Madame d'Orselis, "men do not like uniformity." "If that is
the case," added the chevalier, "anyone who has the honor to court you

will not get bored with you." There was no one who failed to smile upon seeing that he was starting to figure out the true character of his new beloved: she blushed with anger at this; but since she is very intelligent and since she did not want to discourage a man who was preventing her from feeling bored, she replied in a rather playful tone, and turning toward Madame d'Arcire, she said to her, "And you, madam, will you not tell us anything about everything that has happened to you?" "If one begins to live," she rejoined, "only when one's heart is touched, my story would be too short." She turned to the marquis with long glances upon finishing these few words, which could not apply to the count, since this relationship had been going on for two years. The comment seemed to carry enormous weight in the mouth of a reasonable woman: Brésy remained as if bewitched by it; the count smiled bitterly; and I proposed a stroll in order to draw everyone out of a state of embarrassment. Each couple paired off as they pleased: the count insisted on strolling with me; Madame d'Arcire gave us an uneasy look; the chevalier and Madame d'Orselis went off down a walkway shaded by trees; Brésy wanted to follow the marquise; but she, ashamed of the speech that she had just made, and perhaps fearing to receive thanks from a man whom she did not want to have any obligation to her, told him that she needed rest because of her headache and that for this, she needed to be alone. He remained with the old duke, and I told the count that I absolutely insisted on having an explanation with the marquise; that she believed me to be her rival: that this was the main plot complication; that it would come to a tragic ending, and I would not rest until I had brought her out of her error.

"You hardly know your own sex if you do not understand that the only way to make Madame d'Arcire come back to me is to cause her jealousy," he replied; "you have just seen an example of that in the chevalier's adventure." "Yes, but she will hate me," I replied; "I have no intention of becoming your victim." "Come on," Selincourt told me, laughing, "you will be included in the peace treaty." While we were having that conversation, we made our way, without realizing it, toward the wood: I had never seen it before; and since it is delightful, owing to the fountains of various shapes, and to the marvelous marble statues located at the end of all the walkways, I traversed a part of this agreeable place with the count; but while crossing it from one side to the other, I spotted the marquise reclining on a grassy area adjacent to the palisade on the side where we were. "Come, Count," I whispered to Selincourt, "behold an adventure out of a novel; come see your beloved in a posture of distress." He did indeed approach, and looking through the hedge, he saw that she was playing with a cane in a fountain located at her feet, and that she was holding in her other hand a little portrait, the features of which he could not recognize because the branches were too thick. The marquise's face was not turned in our direction. I told the count, without fearing to be over-heard, that he should go and throw himself at her feet, and that a person who had withdrawn from the company in order to come and look at the portrait of a lover who was pretending to be unfaithful certainly deserved to have her heartache assuaged. "Ah!" the count replied to me, "cruel person, where have you led me? You cannot imagine my grief, I am now more capable of taking Brésy's life than ever; it is doubtless his portrait that causes my perfidious lover such concentration; she has never had my portrait, she has always refused to receive it, she has such scruples only for me." I remained very surprised at these words; and noticing some writing tablets on the grassy area, I pulled them through the branches as unobtrusively as possible. The count seized them at once: "here is the means to enlighten us," he told me. Then we quietly moved away from that place, and leafing through the writing tablets, we found this poem:

> *O you, who repay my fond love with disdain,*
> *You, who despite your lack of constancy*
> *Over my soul will always reign,*
> *For one more moment have a thought of me.*
> *For that one moment, set aside . . .*

There was only this fragment on the writing tablets; the pages were even wet in several places. "Well now, Selincourt," I said, "are you not ashamed of your jealousy? To whom could these words be addressed except to you?" "Is it possible that you can be misled by so shabby a pretense?" he interrupted impatiently. "Madame d'Arcire is so sensitive that, if Brésy even glanced at you or the beautiful Orselis ever so briefly, she would have found material for suspicions and reproaches. How obstinate you are in your judgments!" he added, seeing that I was not at all persuaded.

"Do you not see the fire of a new passion burning in this poem? Must the portrait not convince you? And is the weakness of your sex unknown to you?" "I do not know what all this means," I replied. "I see nothing but obscurity in it." "And for my part," the count went on, "I see in it nothing but clear truths that are only too fatal to my love. I adore her, I can love no one but her, she means even more to me when I am losing her. Ah, faithless one!" he added in a louder voice, "was it necessary to do me the favor of coming to my home only in order to cause my death? But I will not be the first to die; my rival, whom you so unjustly prefer to me, will be the first to experience my fury, for I want to deprive you of the means to betray me once grief has put an end to my life." At these words, he insisted on leaving, presumably in order to seek out Brésy, but he saw him pass by with the Duke de . . . quite nearby. "Marquis," he called out to him in a violent tone of voice, "I would like to have a word with you; the duke will agree to it," he added, speaking to his uncle, who let them go off together; but I, being deathly afraid of some fatal outcome, approached the duke: I told him my concerns in a few words, and gave him the task of not letting them out of his sight.

I found out later that the count, upon arriving at Brésy's side, asked him whether he had given his portrait to the Marquise d'Arcire; but it was with so haughty a tone that the marquis did not give him a precise answer. "This is no time for evasiveness," rejoined the count; "I must positively know the truth of this matter." "I am hardly accustomed to being interrogated," Brésy replied coldly; "questions annoy me even more than moralizing puts me to sleep, and besides, I do not believe that such an explanation is necessary." "It is necessary to me to such an extreme degree," said the count, "that I must have it, or else your life in its place." Brésy responded that duels were hardly in fashion, but that he followed fashion only in matters of dress, and immediately drew his sword, the count did likewise, and a bloody scene would have taken place if the duke, who had been following them all along, had not gone to put himself between them. "What are you doing, Selincourt?" he exclaimed with an air of authority that he was able to take with his nephew. "What has made you so furious? Have you forgotten the unpleasant consequences of these sorts of combats? Entrust your concerns to me," he added. "I will resolve them with the marquis in a less drastic manner." The Duke de

. . .'s action and speech had at once put a stop to the eagerness of the two rivals; his high birth and his age made him eligible to be named a marshal of France.[69] They remained a bit ashamed of their angry outburst, and the count, being less in control of himself and more distressed, went back into the wood at the very moment that the marquise and I were on our way out of it.

I had gone to find her immediately after I had begged the duke to keep watch over the actions of our lovers; I found her so preoccupied by her reverie, that the noise I made upon arriving was not enough to shake her out of it. "Look," I said to her, "the count is over there in a state of despair; I fear a quarrel; he is with Brésy, and it is you, madam, who are causing the whole misunderstanding." "Me!" cried Madame d'Arcire, thoroughly frightened, "what can you be talking about? And should I not take whatever you tell me as suspect?" "This is no time for doubting, madam," I told her, "two brave men are perhaps dueling at this very moment for the love of you." The marquise shuddered at these words: and running in the direction where I was guiding her, we encountered Selincourt alone, but in a fury that made him turn around as soon as he noticed us. The marquise followed him and soon cut off his path. "Where are you running off to?" she asked him with a gentle and languishing look, and while extending her hand to him in a gracious manner. "I am off to seek out Brésy a second time," he replied, "to make him die at my hand, or to die by his. The Duke de . . . separated us, but nothing further can stop me." "Wait," Madame d'Arcire replied to him; "your injustice is extreme; you seek to kill a man who has not wronged you in my heart, while I am sparing the life of a cruel friend who steals your heart from me." I was so close to the marquise when she finished these words that I opened my arms and embraced her tenderly. "How happy we would all be," I told her, "if Brésy has no more wronged the count than I have wronged you on his account!" Madame d'Arcire is kind and gentle by nature: her tears covered her cheeks at that moment, and as she caressed me in return, she said to me, "Ah, my dear, how much heartache you have caused me!" I wanted to respond; but Selincourt interrupted me in order to ask her for an explanation of the portrait. "Behold," she told him

69. See the Introduction, note 2.

while giving him the box that contained it; "behold, you unjust creature, what rival you sought to exterminate!" The count, looking at this fatal picture in a violent hurry, recognized a portrait of himself that was such a good likeness that, throwing himself at the marquise's feet and embracing them ardently, he felt a thrill of joy so intense that it did not allow him to speak for a very long time. You can well imagine, madam, the effect that such an outcome must produce: people gave frantic explanations and said the sorts of confused things that testify to the feelings of a tender passion better than eloquent speech: and after I had learned from the marquise that she had had Selincourt's portrait made with extraordinary secrecy, in order not to grant him so great a favor as to receive one from him;[70] when, I say, I had learned this particular from her own mouth, I withdrew in order to leave them the freedom to speak without witnesses. They rejoined the company some time later. The count graciously advanced toward Brésy, to whom I had already told a portion of what had just transpired.

"Marquis," he told him, "a mistaken notion that sent me into a consuming rage caused my angry outburst against you just now; I do not by nature like to act like a bully; but since I had lost my head: and since you are one of the most reasonable men in the world and a good friend of mine, I hope that this adventure will make our friendship more closely knit, rather than destroying it." "My word, Count," rejoined Brésy, "in all this business I see myself as the only one mistreated: you picked a quarrel with me, I served to make you learn how greatly you are preferred; your brand of generosity is not difficult to practice: but if the part I play is not an advantageous one," he added, laughing, "at least I must carry it off with aplomb." With those words, he wholeheartedly embraced Selincourt. Madame d'Arcire, who could no longer keep her tender feelings a secret after such an outburst, admitted, while blushing, that she esteemed the count so highly that she would raise no objection to contracting a lifelong engagement with him. Then, turning toward the marquis, she told him: "do not be angry at me for having toyed with you a bit too much; spite and jealousy can sometimes make a person do worse things; and besides, there is no great harm in having behaved toward you

70. See note 57 in the translation, p. 60.

just this once in the same way you have behaved with so many other women."

Brésy, who saw that the understanding between them had been going on for far more than one day, and that it was about to become serious, resigned himself like a gallant man who is hardly in a position to get angry.

The public declaration that the marquise had just made could not fail to be pleasing to her lover and to the Duke de . . . . She is beautiful, young, and rich; there is no couple better matched. Your vengeance is approaching, madam; they will be married in a short time.

You see, madam, that we engaged in heroics during our trip, and that we did not always waste time on trifles. I would have liked to be able to sound the trumpet, in order to relate this adventure to you. It is at least a little bit tragic, madam, although no blood was shed; but I do not like to adopt a tone that I cannot long sustain.

Starting that very day Brésy addressed his amorous attentions to me; thus I was not destined for idleness of the heart. He is conceited; he told me various details about his attachment to Madame d'Arcire which proved to me, either that he is quite vain, or that women make great headway when they want to call a lover back through jealousy. However, you must not carry your ideas too far, madam; but coquettishness always seems to me to be excessive when one is scrupulous about fidelity. Still, let us not condemn anyone, we could fall into the same when our turn comes; and besides, my moralizing is quite out of place, for the count found new charms in the marquise; and since the Marquis de Brésy is very likable, I listened to him obligingly, although not with tenderness at that point.

It was only with regret, and at the last possible moment, that we left the charming house where our lovers had reconciled: we got back into boats, although we were traveling upstream, in order to depart from it less quickly; the night was magnificent; we arrived only at daybreak.

Several days had already passed, in which we were all living in perfect harmony, with the exception of Chanteuil and Madame d'Orselis, who mixed a bit too much discord with their pleasures, when the count proposed a hunting expedition to us for the following day. The weather was suitable for such an excursion: a rain shower had beaten down the dust somewhat, and moderated the heat of the sun; we had all brought hunting attire, elegant and sumptuous: Selincourt had a good pack of hounds for chasing the deer, and some marvelous horses. I am not a very resolute horsewoman; but I sit a horse gracefully: and if I had not had an overly fiery horse, I would have got through reasonably well: but no sooner had he heard that chaotic yet pleasing sound of the dogs, the hunting horns, and the huntsmen than he carried me off in front of the hunting party, and leaving the deer and the hunt, he plunged into the woods on the right with a mettle that I did not have the strength or the skill to stop. I held on to the saddlebow as tightly as I could, and I would have been able to regain hold of the stirrup and steady myself again after that first squall, if a branch of substantial thickness had not struck me in the face, which caused me a horrible pain, which I was unable to withstand, and which was so violent that it ultimately made me fall off. My hair, which had been artfully arranged, became entangled around that branch; I had a lot of it ripped out, which caused extreme pain, my hat was twenty paces away from me; I was uttering piercing cries when I spotted Brésy, who was coming to my aid as fast as his horse could carry him: he had followed my tracks like a true knight, as soon as he had seen my calamity; but he had not been able to intercept me because my horse was heading straight through the woods: he arrived just as my pain was at its most severe. "Ah, mademoiselle," he said to me, "what a dreadful mishap! How unfortunate I am not to have been able to prevent it!" He looked so grieved as he spoke thus, and he showed such sorrow as he saw my hair hanging from that pernicious branch, that I felt genuinely obliged to him. "You did what you could," I told him; "this is the sort of mishap that cannot be foreseen; one would have to be a true stoic to maintain that I am not in great pain at the present moment. My philosophy does not go quite so far," I added, laughing; "but I do feel stoical enough to get back on my horse, however, if you would kindly return to me my hat that is in the thicket." "I do not know whether I ought to render you that service," he answered me. "This solitary spot is quite suitable for declaring to you the feelings that you already know I have." "You would be very unwise to take so unfortunate a moment for such a declaration," I promptly interrupted; "one needs to be of a cheerful and calm frame of mind to listen to such things without taking offense, and I once had a friend who failed to win his ladylove only because he chose the wrong moment." Brésy clearly saw that I was joking; he went to fetch my hat, he adjusted my hairdo, he gave me some lotion[71] to put on the scratches that I had on my face: then, giving twenty blows with a switch to my horse, which had not moved away, he mounted it, after helping me to mount his horse, which he assured me was better behaved than the other. We rejoined the hunting party, and I had the glory of still being present when the deer was killed, despite the condition I was in. Everyone came up to me to commiserate over this mishap; I was praised more than I deserved for my fearlessness. Enough daylight remained when the hunt had finished that the count proposed going to a charming house, located half a league from where we then were. This house has amazing fountains, both of the level and spurting kinds: we did not expect to find any other pleasures there apart from that of strolling: but the count, whose passion was renewed, did not miss any occasion to display the intense joy that he felt at being reunited with his charming beloved. Upon approaching a labyrinth, we heard instruments being tuned, and right after that a beautiful voice sang the following lyrics:

> *Thanks to your loveliness, wherever it may shine,*
> *You make hearts captive at your shrine.*
> *A heart under your sway adores its horrid pain;*
> *In vain did my heart seek to break away;*
> *More enslaved than ever, it comes back to your reign,*
> *Which alone is sweet and glorious to obey.*

The marquise had no doubt that this was a gallant present from the count; she whispered something about it to him. Another voice, just as beautiful as the first, sang a second aria: there was a marvelous chorus, and the whole thing appeared to us as if produced by magic: but we found out later that Selincourt had brought some excellent musicians from Paris, from which city we were less than a day's journey away; that he had written the lyrics, and that a composer of exceptional ability had written the music. We next found a table covered with everything that can satisfy one's tastes: it was at the foot of the lovely waterfalls on the

71. The French specifies *eau de la reine de Hongrie,* a type of smelling salt made from an extract of rosemary, that was used as a cure-all.

grounds of this house. Never were people's minds so disposed to be joyful; and never did one have so perfect a pleasure: nothing disturbed it; we waited for the moon to rise before heading back: the moon was very late, but we did not get bored. While waiting, we took a stroll down a walkway so dark that even the rays of the noonday sun could barely penetrate it. Our company was too numerous for any of us to get frightened by the darkness: and we were thinking only of enjoying ourselves when we saw the figure of a gardener in a white jacket, who was walking several paces in front of us, in one of the parallel walkways. Selincourt called out to him, to learn what he was doing so late in the gardens; the gardener made no answer, and disappeared.

We all ran to seek him in the woods; it was no use. He reappeared a moment later; "this time you will not escape us!" we cried, and we rushed into the parallel walkway, with just as little success. The phantom gardener played this trick on us fully four times: we remained surprised at this, without being frightened by it, and we have been told since that such visions often occur in this place, which formerly belonged to a famous minister.[72] I am telling you, madam, what I saw, and seven people who are not swayed by preconceived ideas could hardly have imagined such a thing if it were not founded on something real. We were so far from being frightened that we remained some further time at the same spot. "It would be sad if this figure of a gardener had the same power as a young lady who has been seen in a district of Normandy," I told them; "she makes people keep traveling until she makes them sick, and sometimes even worse." "How can that be?" said Madame d'Arcire. "Is this a tall tale that you are relating to us?" "No, indeed," I replied; "I heard it from people worthy of belief. That spirit has the appearance of an attractive woman, always mounted on a good horse. People in the region refer to her simply as 'the young lady.'

A poor parish priest, whose mount had been pricked,[73] had business

---

72. If the minister in question is Nicolas Fouquet, Louis XIV's finance minister who had been disgraced in 1661 and would spend the final years of his life in prison, then the château is his spectacular showplace, Vaux-le-Vicomte. Ownership of the property passed to Fouquet's son, who apparently never lived there and may have been willing to let aristocratic visitors use or rent it.

73. His horse's foot had been injured by a nail during shoeing.

in the neighboring village; he went there on foot; the way was not long:
he encountered the young lady, who got him so utterly lost that one
would have said that he had walked on the plant that causes disorienta-
tion. He found his house again only when the lady traveler saw fit: but
he arrived there so exhausted and with a mind so disturbed that he went
straight to bed with a high fever. He declared that the pitiless young lady
would laugh heartily whenever she saw a man become disoriented: the
blood rushed to his brain and he died within three days."

"Oh, as for that, mademoiselle," said the Duke de . . . , "you are just
as cruel as that woman, for having killed off that poor parish priest. What
would it have cost you to keep him alive?" "I assure you, Duke, that I
had no power at all over those events," I replied. "I heard this story from
a worthy abbess, whom I would certainly name if I were forced to do
so; and who, since she was in the region when this adventure happened,
surely deserves to be believed."

Everyone remained quite shocked by such a bloodthirsty ghost. The
marquis asked me whether the young lady ever swung her leg over the
saddlebow.[74] "Do not make fun of people who get lost," I told him; "how
do you know whether the route that you are presently taking is reli-
able? Young ladies are sometimes even more adept than sprites at making
men wander off track, for it must be the case that [the young lady of
Normandy] is such a creature." Brésy wanted to answer: but the count,
who was feeling eager to talk, interrupted him to say that he was not
necessarily an unbeliever, and that if he had to follow any philosophical
school, it would be that of the cabalists. "I well know," he added, "that
they are not fashionable, and that one must say *Long live Descartes* in
order to fit in with the majority's taste: but good cabalists believe with
humility in things that prove the immortality of the soul; and in addition
they have many good scientific arguments that prove the possibility of
ghosts."[75] The marquis, who saw that the conversation was taking on a

74. Likely an allusion to the narrator's misfortune during the hunting expedition earlier
in the day.

75. Murat's knowledge of cabalists was derived from Nicholas-Pierre-Henri de Mont-
faucon de Villars's 1670 novel *Le Comte de Gabalis ou Entretiens sur les sciences secretes*.
As opposed to real cabalists, students of an esoteric Jewish mystical tradition, Villars's
protagonist represents occultist groups interested in theosophical speculation, matters

moral tone, which was dampening the count's good spirits, informed us that the moon had already risen some time earlier, and that we needed to take advantage of that. We followed his advice; we got into the carriages that the count had summoned, and we returned to our primary location.

Several days later, an elderly abbé with a very pleasing wit brought along a woman who was madly in love with Brésy: we were made aware of that circumstance that very evening, through her behavior and through the sorrow that she displayed whenever he said a word to me. She was a friend of Selincourt, as was the elderly abbé, who was recovering from a serious illness and who was coming to complete his convalescence in this place, just like cousin Chonchon in the house of Monsieur Bernard.[76]

The very next day we took a day trip to a place several leagues away from the Selincourt estate: Madame de Talemonte (that was this woman's name) and I were together in the marquis's carriage: there was no folding seat; he seated himself between the two of us; and as his inclination often made him turn in my direction, the jealous Talemonte would rudely push him with her elbow: I felt the repercussion from it, and I laughed heartily at the manner in which Brésy was receiving these tokens of tenderness. She has a pleasant enough voice: throughout the trip she constantly sang this aria from *Bellérophon,* which begins with the following words:

> *Despite all my sorrows I would be too happy*
> *If feelings of contempt could cure my love.*[77]

You know, madam, that this opera was then being revived: but she would have resurrected it from even further in the past, for the sake of the parallel she wished to make with her own situation. She was straining her

---

such as restoring human contact with the divine and promoting world peace and a single world religion. One such secret society, the Rosicrucians, appears to have been operating in Paris as of around 1622. Obviously this type of thinking was alien to the thoroughgoing rationalism of Descartes, which by century's end had influenced many of the salons.

76. Monsieur Bernard is the protagonist of Florent Dancourt's one-act comedy *La Maison de Campagne* (The Country House; 1688) whose home is constantly invaded by unwelcome visitors.

77. In *Bellérophon* (1679), an opera by Thomas Corneille and Bernard le Bovier de Fontenelle with music by Lully, the jealous and vindictive Sténobée, who sings this passage, suffers likewise from unrequited love (act I, scene I).

lungs with such pathos-filled singing, if one can call it that. The marquis responded poorly to it; but I believe I noticed shortly thereafter that she got her revenge. I do not know whether he is among those easily touched by demonstrations of affection, or whether the small amount of hope that I was giving him made him settle for a surer match: but I saw Madame de Talemonte quite content with herself and with him; and she believed she had an enormous superiority over me, even though I still appeared to be the marquis's more serious passion. I must not lie to you, madam, I was aware that I was beginning to have feelings for him: the small amount of attention that he was devoting to that woman did not fail to bother me; and I resolved on a small bit of revenge that worked out successfully for me, as I will shortly tell you. On the other hand, the elderly abbé felt the desires of his youth reawaken in this place; he assured Madame de Talemonte that she would find a heart ready to serve her whenever she pleased. You can easily judge how this offer was received; she even made jokes about it. The abbé was beside himself with anger; he figured out the ingrate's schemes and pestered her with bantering for the whole time she remained with us.

The marquis, who was not in love with her, and who is not known for discretion, entered into everything like a man who is weary of tokens of passion, and he decided to make a confession to me of his weaknesses and of Talemonte's excesses. I did not reproach him for anything, but one evening when both of us were under a bower of honeysuckle and the group reminded me of the promise that I had made to relate some of my adventures, I seized upon the occasion, and I began to speak as follows.

"I am not very wise, ladies, to launch out into a recital of what I ought to hide even from myself: it is hardly proper for a young lady[78] to admit that her heart has been touched: even when her feelings have not exceeded the bounds of strict decorum, it is always considered excessive to have had such feelings: but fortunately I am not dealing with overly severe judges," I continued, smiling; "and I would unduly bore you, if I only related to you my feelings of indifference.

---

78. The narrator is the only woman in the group who has not been married. According to social norms, she thus cannot speak about her love interests, past or present, with the same freedom as the other women.

So, ladies, I fell in love with a very charming man, at least he seemed so to me, and perhaps even that went too far: he had acquired a hold over my heart in a rather short time, because his passion had appeared completely sincere to me. Hardly had he learned the attachment I felt for him when I found myself opposed by a woman of the sort that do not get easily discouraged and who, since they do not have very strict morals, believe that it is permitted to do anything in order to conquer a rebellious heart. This woman was not ugly; she was even somewhat intelligent. Alcandre,[79] for you will allow me to refer to him by the first fictional name that comes to mind, a man whom I want to portray accurately; Alcandre, then, held out without faltering against his new ladylove's assaults: he scoffed at them in an insulting manner: it was at my feet that he would come to seek refuge from her pursuit of him. I did not allow him to witness anything of what was happening within my heart: I let my rival express jealousy, and she naturally had more of it to feel than I did; and I would ridicule myself whenever I caught myself experiencing the least pang of it in myself; but men have just a limited degree of constancy."

I must interrupt myself, madam, to tell you that the marquis was staring wide-eyed as he listened to me, as if he had been able to guess how this adventure would turn out; torn between fear of having a beloved rival, hope of being the hero of the story, and sorrow for having displeased me, he was not sure what kind of countenance to maintain. I took pleasure in his uneasiness, and I continued my narrative as follows. "So here you have, ladies, the beginning of an adventure, whose outcome you presumably cannot guess. Alcandre had not spent more than four days with his new ladylove when remorse over his infidelity strongly tormented him; he resorted to a sincere confession of his mistake. He came to me to make that confession with such a show of repentance that I forgave him for a fickleness that perhaps would make him less likely to succumb to similar

---

79. Alcandre was also the main character of the anonymous *L'imagination détrompée ou la phantasie débrouillée au sujet de l'amoureux imaginaire* (Imagination Set Straight or Fantasy Resolved on the Subject of the Imaginary Lover; 1675). In this novel a select salon company similarly congregates in a country château to tell stories and to deliberate on a variety of theosophical topics, including the utility of organized religion, the existence of ghosts, and the relationship among visions, dreams, and supernatural beings.

lapses in the future; but since I had suffered from it and I wanted a bit of revenge for my relief, I chose my rival as the object of that vengeance, rather than my lover. I recounted to that woman her own story and mine using unfamiliar names: she became pale, but I do not know whether she improved her behavior. As for Alcandre, he appeared to me so content when I had finished my narration that I applauded myself for having kept him in suspense and for seeing that I had not made a bad choice."[80]

I must confess, madam, that I was very wicked to tell in this way, before this woman, an episode that would cause her so much shame: but please forgive me, I got too much pleasure from it to be capable of feeling any remorse over it. She did not know how to take such an allegory: she bit her lips, she stuck out her chest; she opened her mouth to speak; but the looks of collusion between the marquis and myself revealed to her that she was not in the stronger position: so the poor woman, beside herself with rage, told us over supper that she wanted to return home the following day. The abbé was in no mood to follow her whims, and that one in particular; but this woman, who remembered having heard Brésy say that he needed to make a trip to Paris, turned toward him and asked him, in a tone of voice that was indignant and pleading at the same time, whether he would be willing to give her the pleasure of taking her with him: "My heavens no, madam," he answered; "I still have a few things to attend to in this place." The manner in which he spoke these few words was so amusing that we all burst out laughing, and that put the final touch on the disconsolate lover's confusion. Selincourt, who was in his own home, felt obliged to be the first to resume a serious tone: he begged her to remain for a few more days. I entreated the marquis not to refuse her request. He answered me jokingly, and Talemonte did not especially like my interceding; but since I found it amusing to prolong this scene, I urged Brésy so much that finally he felt stung by my eagerness to send him away with my rival, and he pledged to take her home. In fact, this was truly done in a manner that could not have given her much satisfaction; still, she did not fail to triumph. And since I have pledged to give you an exact account of everything that happened to us, I had no sooner

---

80. The narrator refers to her choice of Alcandre, who by his reaction to her story has proven himself a worthy lover.

succeeded in my endeavor than I was sorry for it. Brésy came over to my side. "You have insisted on it, mademoiselle," he said to me. "I will take Madame de Talemonte home, I will leave with her if you wish. I had flattered myself by the end of your narrative that I was not so indifferent to you that you would subject me to an adventure like this; but either you have wanted to deceive me, or else I have deceived myself." "You will not be committed to anything against your wishes," I answered him, laughing, though I felt little desire to laugh; "people are weak only when they want to be." "Ah, mademoiselle!" he replied, "when one's heart is even slightly sensitive, one fears everything, and I clearly see that you have more love for yourself than tenderness for another." "Leave me," I then told him; "I do not know how I can allow you to speak to me in that tone of voice," I continued, "but I must blame no one but myself. A foolish plan that I imagined in order to make fun of an outrageous woman has made you infer things that I had no thought of."

The manner in which I spoke these final words should have either pleased Brésy infinitely, or mortally offended him. I did not know what effect they had produced upon him; but the following day I received a letter from my mother, asking me to return to Paris for a ceremony that she wished me to attend, and she asked me to go to meet her at once in the carriage of one of her ladies-in-waiting, along with a servant girl who was attending me. The marquis, who had had time to reflect during the night on everything that I had said to him, and who had a high opinion of his own merit, concluded that I had doubtlessly spoken out of spite. He was grateful that I felt as I did, and tried to persuade me to depart with Talemonte and him. On my end, I was dying with eagerness to do so, and I had my mother's order to justify me: I felt a fondness for Brésy; he was indeed a very suitable match for me. That could evolve into a serious relationship; but I had felt such stinging heartache by the fact that he had obeyed my words rather than my feelings that I did not want to contradict myself. He got down on his knees before me to entreat me to grant him this favor: he proposed to me that, if I refused his request, he would stay with us and only give his carriage to Talemonte; but I was unyielding, though very upset to be doing so. One acts bizarrely, madam, when one goes as far as to be even slightly touched by love; for you can clearly see that I did not know precisely what I wanted. Finally the moment of departure arrived; I had several more assaults to withstand. Madame d'Arcire told me that I was foolish; Selincourt joked with me about it; the chevalier and Madame d'Orselis, who were getting along quite well at this point, condemned my conduct.

Poor Talemonte during this time was playing an unpleasant role, but the hope of soon exchanging it for a better one consoled her in advance. She even had the courage to withstand a last attempt on the part of the marquis to make me come along, or else to oblige me to agree that he remain. He was already in his carriage with her; he called over one of his valets who was on horseback; he sent the man to me to learn my final decision. "Go on, mademoiselle," the count told me, "go on, you will come back in two days; you will satisfy your mother, you will do a service to Brésy, and you will spare yourself the distress that you are going to feel when they are a hundred paces away from here." I was already feeling the truth in this prediction; but I remained firm to the end, and I proudly sent word that it was a waste of time to take so many useless measures. I gave a letter to one of his servants, in which I sent word to my mother that I was not feeling very well, and that I asked her to forgive me if I did not obey her.

It is true, madam, that I felt an extreme distress as soon as they had gone too far away to turn back: I suffered cruelly from it, and all the more so because I wanted to hide my feelings, and I did it so well that I was accused of insensitivity rather than of weakness: but to you, to whom I hide nothing, I admit that I spent two wretched nights; however, they were still more pleasant than the days, because at least then I was not hiding my feelings.

I will quickly skip over those two days of absence: we took walks, we played cards, and on the third day we saw the marquis arrive. I cannot properly tell you which emotion was stronger in my heart, joy or shame; it was a confused mixture of them, which nevertheless had its own kind of sweetness. Brésy displayed all the ardor of a genuine passion, and all the submissiveness of a man who feels a bit guilty. People were looking at us in a manner that made me exasperated; but finally they took pity on the marquis, and they left him a few moments to sort things out with me. So we made up, madam, or rather we began our mutual understanding; for until Madame de Talemonte arrived, I did not believe that my feelings had advanced so far: so true it is that jealousy has a decisive effect. Brésy spoke to me with the tone of voice that one must use with a young noblewoman who is virtuous, but who, not being a child, wants to get to know her husband before marrying him. I gave way to the pleasure that one has in speaking about oneself, and I will not tell you anything more about that except in passing, until the end of our trip.

Selincourt continued to enjoy the most perfect happiness: he asked Madame d'Arcire to complete the poem that she had started in her writing tablets; she did so on the spot; therefore, I will not guarantee to you that the verses are very good.

> *O you, who repay my fond love with disdain,*
> *You, who despite your lack of constancy*
> *Over my soul will always reign,*
> *For one more moment have a thought of me;*
> *For that one moment, set all thought aside*
> *Of the nymph who recently has set your heart on fire.*
> *Despite my fierce wrath my passion has not died,*
> *Nor has my love snuffed out my ire.*
> *If you employ this precious moment properly,*
> *You will come back to me; my heart feels sure.*
> *Elsewhere, you might find more charms easily;*
> *But where will you find a tenderness so pure*
> *And solely by its excess reckoned properly?*
> *Ah, Tircis, I alone of women here below*
> *Can give you, without harming modesty,*
> *Pleasures that, through my zeal and constancy,*
> *Are lasting and can charm you so.*

"There is a bit of vanity here," said Madame d'Arcire as she gave him back the writing tablets, "but poets are normally accused of being vain. However, I reply that I am not stating anything that I am not able to maintain." "Yes, you charming person," Selincourt answered her, thanking her profusely, "you are indeed the only woman with whom I can live happily." You can easily judge, madam, that a conversation in that mode could be long without being boring; therefore, they did not finish

it until servants came to tell them that we were about to sit down to dinner. The chevalier and Madame d'Orselis were also in a calm state; and
I listened very willingly to everything that Brésy wanted to tell me. Even
the kindly duke did not fail to contribute to our pleasures; he sought to
be agreeable to me, and his love was not yet violent enough to make him
jealous; and his rivals, until that point, had given him nothing more than
a slight competition, without inspiring jealousy. We still had some time
to spend on Selincourt's estate: every day he sought out new pleasures;
he proposed one to us that could be called a pleasure only through the
oddity of the individuals whom he wanted to show us. We were all in that
predisposition to joy that makes all things either more attractive or more
ridiculous than they really are. One day we dined early in order to have
more time. We departed in two carriages and we arrived, after one hour
on the road, near a château with a drawbridge. It is true that this item
was quite useless, since the moats were almost completely filled in. Madame de Richardin, mistress of the domain, housed, within a small and
very badly formed body, a soul that aspired to high rank: anything that
represented the nobility made her thrill with joy. We had to get out of our
carriages before crossing the bridge because the gate was so low and so
narrow that, as far back as anyone could remember, no vehicle had ever
been seen to pass through it. The desire to laugh seized us as soon as we
reached the courtyard: the building is antiquated, with a large quantity
of towers. But the incomparable Madame de Richardin was still building
new towers, in order to add to the antiquity and in order to persuade
people that she was descended from the ancient owners of that château.[81]
It was not an easy thing to persuade people of: she and her husband had
bought it two or three years ago:[82] they had even added the particle *de*

81. Descendants of the feudal nobility comprised one of the smallest and most elite
noble classes. In purchasing a medieval château and in seeking to augment its antiquity
by constructing additional towers, used for defense of the fiefdom in medieval times,
Madame de Richardin attempts to link her husband's family to that of the château's
original owners.

82. Titles of nobility were often usurped by nonnobles during the sixteenth and seventeenth centuries through the purchase of feudal estates. By "living nobly" on these estates—refraining from manual and commercial activities and obtaining exemption from
official taxation—wealthy families from the commercial classes could eventually come

and the suffix *din* to their name, which, deprived of those ornaments, was originally just Richard: a name that had been imposed upon the father of Monsieur de Richardin, because in fact he was a very rich merchant.[83] Selincourt hastily gave us an account of those particulars. We composed our faces in order to make our entrance like sensible people: but we nearly lost our equanimity when we saw Monsieur de Richardin come to meet us. He was a short man, dark-complexioned and dried out, with flat hair, a pinchina[84] outfit, waxed shoes like slippers, and a tie of black taffeta, because his wife said that it gave him a warlike appearance.[85] Mademoiselle de Richardin was right behind her father: she is two feet taller than he is and could make a fine halberdier[86] in the French guards: she is stout in proportion to her height, her skin is of a reddish-brown color, and she speaks in a falsetto voice by order of her mother, in order to make her seem younger. Hardly had we recovered from the surprise that such a greeting had caused us, when we noticed the true Madame de Richardin lying upon a daybed at the far end of the room, dressed in a gris-de-lin[87] and silver dressing gown. This posture could not hide a hump that extended over her right side. Her face is long, narrow and pointed; her eyes are small and hollow, her mouth is flat, and her whole body is shaped in such a way that it would cause laughter in persons

---

to be seen as noble. Although this transformation generally took at least two to three generations to take effect, the de Richardins have only owned their estate for two or three years. See also note 33.

83. Although the nobiliary particle "de" was used to distinguish between noble and nonnoble names, the use of such particles was not strictly controlled by the French state. As such, they could be appropriated by nonnobles to denote a place of origin or even a family lineage without legal consequences. The "de Richardin" family is too foolish to realize, in their desire to speed the ennobling process by modifying their name, that they have achieved the opposite effect: as "Richard" was an old and inelegant word to designate a rich man, the altered name betrays their real origins.

84. An untwilled wool fabric that was made locally.

85. Another effort on the part of Madame de Richardin to manipulate noble signifiers, as nobles had an obligation to defend the king in exchange for the right to hunt, wear a sword, obtain a coat of arms, and possess a fief.

86. A low-ranking soldier who carried a pike in order to attack the cavalry. The position of halberdier was accessible to nonnoble social classes.

87. A reddish white color, viewed as a symbol of constancy in love.

more serious than we. That day her hair was swept up in a portraitlike headdress, full of gold and green ribbons. Her hands, which are large and dried out, were laden with rings; and she was wearing a cross more suited to placing over a bedstead than to wearing around one's neck. I was overcome with such a desire to laugh, and I saw in the eyes of our entire company something so amusing, that I received a considerable relief upon seeing a false step made by the Duke de . . . , which, after making him stumble, sent him staggering several paces away from us, where he bit the dust. We rushed to his side to see whether he was hurt; but he had only been startled; and so we took this pretext to laugh with all our strength. Madame de Richardin did her duty very well and [as she smiled] showed us her teeth, quite black and very long, which was the final step in making her so ridiculous that we were confirmed in the design to make a fool out of her. This required just one step; her ego is gigantic, one can get her to believe anything by means of praising her. I was bold enough to maintain that she appeared as tall as a goddess, or even as the Princess de Conti.[88] Brésy assured her that in all the centuries past one could hardly find a beauty worthy of being compared to her. You can easily imagine that poor Helen of Troy,[89] who must be exhausted with such comparisons, was cited on this occasion. "As for me," said Selincourt, "being fortunate enough to have met Madame de Richardin before you did, I have always thought that Venus could not come close to her charms." "But on whom," rejoined Madame d'Orselis, "will we find hands equal to those which we now see?" "I have always heard it said," rejoined Madame de Richardin, making incomparable facial expressions, "that I have hands formed rather like those of the queen mother,[90] whose were, doubtless, the most beautiful in her kingdom." "I am old enough," said the duke, "to have seen them often: they did not come close to yours." "And the feet," interrupted Chanteuil, seeing that she was stretching out a long and flat one, enclosed in a green silk stocking with gold hems and a silver

---

88. Reference to the novel's dedicatee. See note 1 in the translation, p. 23.

89. Helen, wife of King Menelaus of Sparta, was abducted by the Trojan prince Paris, thus causing the Trojan War. She was typically cited as a model for female beauty.

90. Anne of Austria, mother of King Louis XIV, died in 1666. If the duke had really known her, he would indeed be quite old.

and gris-de-lin backless slipper; "and the feet," he repeated, "did Thetis[91]
ever have any that were similar?"

The little fool, during that time, was looking at the marquis with
an extreme attention: it was a look worthy of being painted. We do not
know whether his figure pleased her more than that of the others, or
whether his praises were more to her taste; but it is certain that he was
preferred, and that after our riotous flatteries, it was to him that she addressed her words. "People have always flattered me," she said, "as having
some beauty: they have never disputed my claims to elegance or grace;
but, sir, that tall creature over there," she added, pointing to her daughter, "has sometimes made my youthfulness open to question; however,
such as you see her, she is only ten years old: I was married at twelve,
and I bore her in the first year of my marriage; but a figure like that one
always harms a reputation, and there are a thousand silly people who
believe that I am fully thirty years old because she is my daughter." "Your
daughter, madam!" exclaimed Brésy, laughing like a madman, "that cannot be: mademoiselle appears to be your grandmother. I beg her pardon
for my sincerity; but can one be master of one's words when one is no
longer master of one's heart?" He finished these words while looking at
her with languishing eyes: the poor little woman was overcome by it. We
saw her get up to our great astonishment, for her figure was even more
contorted standing up than lying down. "Come, marquis," she told him,
"come, let's move into my cabinet,[92] I want to show you my portrait made
when I got married; and also I have some little pieces in verse that will
prove to you that my wit is hardly inferior to my body." The poor Brésy
no longer felt a desire to laugh on hearing this terrifying proposition;
and, taking the most polite tone that was possible for him, he said: "I
believe, madam, that these ladies will be delighted to follow you." "These
ladies are free to do what they wish," she rejoined; "come anyway." "But,

91. In classical mythology, Thetis was a very beautiful sea goddess and the beloved of
Jupiter, who married her to his grandson, Peleus. The reference to her feet is perhaps a
deliberate confusion with the heel of her son, Achilles, that was the only vulnerable spot
in the body of that great hero.

92. A private room adjacent to the bedchamber designed to serve as a retreat. These
rooms were often furnished with books and works of art and could be used as studies. See
note 19 in the translation, p. 29.

madam," he said to her in a tone slightly above a whisper, "what will Monsieur de Richardin say?" "Monsieur de Richardin," she interrupted impatiently, "is not accustomed to bothering me; he is speaking to the duke about their first military campaigns." It is true that they had started a conversation; but it was far from revolving around war; poor Monsieur de Richardin had never known anything about that subject except what he had learned of it in the gazette.[93]

The way that Madame de Richardin was taking the matter did not permit the marquis to wait for further urging; he had to follow her. We remained in wonderment and surprise over this little monster's way of acting. It had been less than a quarter of an hour that poor Brésy was with his new conquest, when we heard screams like those of a madwoman. We rushed over to the door of the cabinet, and saw the unfortunate Brésy sitting in an armchair looking rather well, but in a motionless state that was pretending to be a faint: the desperate little woman ran up to him and eagerly tried to help him. He got up abruptly, apologizing to us for the state in which he appeared in front of ladies, and assured us that he was rather prone to such attacks. Madame de Richardin asked for refreshments to be brought for him: we screamed at the top of our lungs; no one appeared. "Why don't you have house bells?" the duke said to her. "It's because," she replied, "my ancestors, who, not to be vain, were quite great lords, didn't have any, and one must always have personal valets within earshot." "You see," added Brésy, "that the personal valets are at fault, and that the screams of your daughter are doing no good." "Ah, marquis," she rejoined, "I see indeed that you are condemning me to have house bells: I will have some tomorrow assuredly." During this time the poor girl was running throughout the château, for she and her father were much afraid of Madame de Richardin; at last a chambermaid came, sunburnt and embarrassed, to ask what people wanted. Madame de Richardin vainly made a huge commotion, in order for her personal valets and majordomo to be found: there had never been any in the house, and the unfortunate

93. Another reference to the dubiousness of Monsieur de Richardin's claims to aristo-cratic status. Being of bourgeois origin rather than a descendant of the older and more prestigious sword nobility, he has clearly not participated in military campaigns, as have the other male characters.

chambermaid knew no more about the meaning of those terms than Andrée in *The Countess d'Escarbagnas* did about the meaning of saucers.[94] She opened her eyes wide and did not answer a word. Madame de Richardin replied to herself, stating that those servants had apparently gone to a nearby city for provisions that she had ordered, and added that the supper, such as could be provided, should be brought in. Soon after the same woman was seen again, accompanied by a little lackey dressed in red, the two of them carrying a rabbit pâté and a big bowl of milk. "Let's sit down at the table," the mistress of the château said boldly; "another time we will have something better." You will perhaps be surprised, madam, that a woman in the country dressed in a silver and gris-de-lin garment, with her hair in a fancy arrangement with jewels, should be so inadequately furnished with servants, and have nothing better to offer for supper; but such is our heroine: she spares no expense for anything that she believes must make her more beautiful, and she has no concern for all the rest.[95]

We sat down at table; but it was not to eat: we must except from that statement Monsieur de Richardin and his daughter, who, charmed to see Madame de Richardin busy, were eating like famished people who wanted to profit from the occasion. When the food from the light meal was removed, I proposed playing small games; for I was unable to be serious. Everyone proposed a game according to his or her fashion; but Madame d'Arcire said that if we wanted to do a proverb play,[96] she would be one of the performers. We agreed to that: we went off as a group in order to plan the manner in which it would be necessary to perform it. When we had agreed on everything, we found that we needed only four performers. It was I, madam, who opened the play with the duke, who

94. Allusion to the one-act comedy by Molière (1671) in which the silly and pretentious owner of a provincial manor uses elegant terms to suggest that she possesses objects or servants she does not really have such as saucers, the mention of which baffles her maid, Andrée.

95. Monsieur de Richardin has had to renounce his commercial activities in order to become ennobled, and the financial consequences of this decision may explain their shortage of servants and of proper food.

96. This is a short play, normally improvised, that illustrates a well-known proverb but without mentioning that proverb in the text; the audience would have to guess it. See also the Introduction.

graciously agreed to be part of our group. He played the part of the chevalier's valet: I was the companion of the marquise, who in the play was to be an elderly woman in love: what follows will inform you about the rest. So just imagine, if you please, that you see me in place of Mademoiselle Beauval and the Duke de . . . in place of La Thorillière.[97] My character was named Catos; the duke's was named Champagne; the marquise's was called Madame de Vieillardis, and Chanteuil's was named simply the Chevalier.[98]

CATOS: Monsieur Champagne, to be frank, you have a very rash master: does he think that he can say sweet nothings to Madame de Vieillardis with impunity? She catches on fire more easily than other women: her husband is her very obedient servant, he would not dream of contradicting her; and even if he took the risk of doing so, it would be a waste of effort; she has a natural inclination toward love, which reaching age sixty and having borne twenty heirs for the house of Vieillardis have done nothing but increase thus far.

CHAMPAGNE: Oh, I certainly believe that, Mademoiselle Catos: I have always heard connoisseurs say that love gets stronger in women's hearts as they get older: it would be a wonderful thing if that were equally true of men; but unfortunately that is not the case; and that is why elderly women in love find lovers only when they have lots of money on hand.

CATOS: Yes; but Madame de Vieillardis believes that she was created by the Graces, and that the handiwork of those goddesses never goes bad. People flatter her every day at close range, in order to make fun of her; and her huge ego makes her accept as genuine everything that is said to her in that manner.

CHAMPAGNE: You must admit, Mademoiselle Catos, that woman is a dreadful machine, and . . .[99]

97. Celebrated comic actors of the period, both of whom had started their careers in Molière's troupe. Jeanne Beauval specialized in soubrette parts; Pierre Lenoir, sieur de La Thorillière, had by this time come to specialize in comic valet parts.

98. In aristocratic Parisian households, male servants were sometimes called by the name of the province in which they were born (hence the name "Champagne"). The name "Vieillardis" is parodically derived from the word *vieille* ("old woman").

99. Parodic allusion to the philosophy of Descartes, who believed that animals are entirely devoid of reason and are in fact machines. In traditional misogynistic discourse, women were equated with animals.

CATOS: Be quiet, Champagne; I do not like science; as soon as I hear anyone speak of machines I run away, or I put my fingers in my ears.

CHAMPAGNE: However, I really had a little scientific exposé to deliver to you, and the strong feelings that I have in my heart would serve me to prove to you that . . .

CATOS: Oh, once again, be quiet! Besides, my lady is coming this way.

MME DE VIEILLARDIS: Good day, my poor Champagne; where's your master today?

CHAMPAGNE: Madam, I thought he was at your side: he must have very serious business for him to separate himself from you for a moment. Indeed, he must have good reason to do so; beautiful and young as you are, where could he be happier?

MME DE VIEILLARDIS: Alas, my poor friend, men are bizarre! It is true that I am beautiful, that's something quite obvious to the sight; and when one's only thirty, I believe that one can still pass for young.

CATOS *aside:* Yet her daughter is forty-five.

MME DE VIEILLARDIS: What's that, Catos?

CATOS: I am saying, madam, that it is most dreadfully wrong for your daughter to look like forty-five.

MME DE VIEILLARDIS: Oh for shame, Catos, let's not speak of her; that's something that I have never understood, when I see the appearance she has. For, indeed, once again, I'm only thirty years old at most; that's an established fact. But I espy the chevalier. Come closer, little rogue, come closer; we have not seen you yet today.

CHEVALIER [*entering*]: I am the one principally punished for it, madam, since I have not seen you; that is a cruel absence: and when one reenters your house, one is always so dazzled by the new graces one finds in you and by the sparkle of your eyes, that one indeed feels that only force of habit can make one withstand both of them.

MME DE VIEILLARDIS: However, I am quite obliging toward you: I try to moderate what there might be of excessive sparkle in my eyes; but love adds fire to them, even when I cut back on their flashing.

CHEVALIER: Why, you keep getting wittier all the time, madam! I am too fortunate to be able to contemplate your beauties at all times, and to enjoy the charms of your divine conversations! But do not refuse me your beautiful hand, to assure me that you will never cut off my freedom to see you.

MME DE VIEILLARDIS: Here it is, Chevalier; can one refuse you anything?

CHEVALIER *kissing the hand of Madame de Vieillardis:* What a hand! Who at this very moment could be as happy as I am? But I see there a ring of which I am jealous: it has the pleasure of touching your fingers: assuredly, it will not stay there; and I am going to make it pass into my hands, to punish it for the excess of sweetness that it has enjoyed.

MME DE VIEILLARDIS: You little wag, there you go, I am giving it to you: it costs two hundred pistoles;[100] but that's a trifle; and I have to converse with you in private about more interesting matters. Let's move into my cabinet. [*Exit*]

CHEVALIER *to Champagne, as he leaves:* Ah, Champagne, I am dying of fright!

CHAMPAGNE *laughing:* In your opinion, Mademoiselle Catos, what will Madame de Vieillardis converse with my master about?

CATOS: Oh! How should I know? About marriage, perhaps; perhaps also about science.[101]

CHAMPAGNE: How's that? About marriage! But doesn't she have a husband?

CATOS: Yes; but she always thinks that he is going to die soon: in any case, it will always be about some such subject that she will converse with him.

MME DE VIEILLARDIS [*reenters hastily*]: Catos, Champagne, help! Bring some smelling salts, some vinegar![102]

CATOS: Oh my God! What on earth is going on?

MME DE VIEILLARDIS: This poor boy loves me with a delicacy so extreme that, at the mere avowal of the passion that I have for him, he fainted away at my feet.

CATOS: Oh, is that all? I thought that everything was lost. I am not astonished by this sudden malady: there is no one who would not fall to the floor after such a declaration.

---

100. A gold coin worth eleven pounds, roughly between $375 and $500 by today's standards.

101. Perhaps another parodic reference to Descartes.

102. Another reference to *eau de la reine de Hongrie;* see note 71 in the translation, p. 86.

MME DE VIEILLARDIS: I am going to look for an excellent elixir that wards off fainting spells. [*Exit*]

CHAMPAGNE: Sir, come out; there is no one here but Mademoiselle Catos and myself.

CHEVALIER: My word, without my fainting fit, I don't know what would have become of me. No one will ever catch me doing that again in my life.

CHAMPAGNE: Good gracious, sir, I too found you very foolhardy to go endure a tête-à-tête with someone like Madame de Vieillardis.

CHEVALIER: In truth I was quite scared of it: but a diamond worth two hundred pistoles, which I had so subtly moved from her finger to mine, deserved a bit of obliging behavior. Even so, I won't risk adventures like that again.

CATOS: My word, sir, leave quickly; for she has gone off to seek an elixir suitable for recovering one's strength. After that you would not be permitted to faint a second time.

CHEVALIER: Farewell, Catos; I'm fleeing to avoid her return. [*Exit with Champagne*]

CATOS: The old woman will be very surprised when she finds that the fainted man is no longer here!

MME DE VIEILLARDIS *reentering:* Catos, where's the chevalier?

CATOS: We revived him, madam, and at once he departed with his man Champagne, who had a lot of difficulty in dragging him. He is so ashamed by this mishap that he says he will never again dare to appear before you.

MME DE VIEILLARDIS: Alas, poor child, how good-hearted he is! Here, my dear Catos, is a bottle that I wouldn't give away for a hundred thousand ecus.[103] Had he taken a drop of the liquid that it contains he would have been cured at once. Call one of my servants, so that I may send off for news of him, while waiting for my horses to be hitched to my carriage, to go myself to get information about him.

Anyone other than old Madame Richardin would have thrown us out of the windows after this insolent proverb play; but she, confident of her youth and beauty, was the first to criticize old Madame Vieillardis,

---

103. A silver coin normally worth three pounds. Today one hundred thousand ecus would be worth approximately fifteen million dollars.

and to say that there is nothing so dreadful as an old woman in love. Brésy guessed our proverb, which was: *He who is afraid of leaves should not go into the forest.* He no longer appeared ill; for he was laughing quite thoughtlessly. Madame de Richardin told him that he was hardly obliging, to show so much merriment at the moment when he was about to leave her. He assured her that he would come back to see her the next day; and we left after taking enough of this pleasure never to come back to it for the rest of our lives: for, as you know, madam, the brief moments when ridiculous things entertain us are followed by an extreme tedium when one continues to witness them. We found ourselves more comfortable at Selincourt after this excursion. How enjoyable things were for several days! And how inappropriately the old duke's amorous fury came along to disturb such sweet calm! It is true that such passion is not all bad; and if I had nothing to tell you but happy things, the rest of my trip would appear quite insipid to you. While we were in this state of mutual understanding, of which I have just told you, and while the duke had not yet reached the point of discovering whether there was any secret collusion between the marquis and me, we would look every day for new excursions and new pleasures, in order to vary our amusements. I have always liked brooks: we were told that there was one at a quarter of a league from the Selincourt estate, the loveliest in the world, and whose source, which issued from a boulder, was shaded by tall trees. We resolved to go there the following day: we found the branches of those trees curved into a bower and surrounded by chains of carnations, orange-flowers and jasmine. There were grassy areas very suitable for sitting all around the bower; and the banks of the stream were adorned with crystal saucers and porcelain platters laden with all kinds of beverages, liqueurs, and ices. Baskets filled with figs, apricots, and peaches, of perfect beauty, were placed between the saucers: and all that produced so beautiful and so brilliant an effect that our astonishment prevented us from eating for a long time. "Who is the fairy," I asked upon arriving in this place that had been made so charming; "who is the good fairy who takes such trouble to entertain us?" "It must be a sorcerer," added the duke, certain that it was the count who was offering this gallant present to the marquise. "What does it matter?" said Brésy; "it is quite evident that no one desires to poison us: it is perhaps the god of the fountain," he added laughing;

"for I do not see many servants to attend the ladies." "That is a very well arranged event," said Selincourt; "I wish I were the one who thought of it." "It is true," replied the chevalier, "that the thing is simple; but what great refinement in its presentation!" The ladies took some cups of ice cream, while praising the charming way things were decorated. The beautiful Orselis was upset to learn that the organizer was not Chanteuil. The marquise would have preferred to be beholden to her suitor for this event. My heart told me that the marquis was the organizer, and that turned out to be true: he had entrusted the matter to his personal valet, who was very skillful at these sorts of things, and who executed them as I have just told you.

After we had consumed some of these liqueurs and eaten some of the fruits, which were excellent and of surprising beauty, the conversation became very lively and very agreeable: the proverb play that we had performed in old Richardin's home inspired in us a taste for that sort of entertainment. We performed one at the edge of the fountain, and in the days following we performed several others at Selincourt. I will not include them here, because that would interrupt my narrative for too long: and moreover, I am obliged to inform you that I had no hand at all in writing the proverb plays that will appear at the end of my trip. They were composed by a person of great intelligence, from whose pen there will shortly appear the story of Madame de Martane.[104] You see, madam, by this admission, that I do not wish to steal any of the glory that belongs to others.

End of the first book.

---

104. The other author is Catherine Bédacier Durand (discussed in the Introduction), who composed the ten proverb comedies appended to the second volume of the novel's original and subsequent eighteenth-century editions. Her novel *La Comtesse de Mortane* (not *Martane*) appeared the same year as *A Trip to the Country.*

A Trip to the Country

{ PART TWO }

*W*hen we had returned to Selincourt, we remembered that there were several of us who had not satisfied the rule that we had imposed on ourselves, namely, to relate some of our adventures; I was excused thanks to the foolish scheme that I had invented in order to vex Madame de Talemonte; and in truth I would have had little to say; it was the Duke de . . . who that evening fulfilled his obligation. He began his speech as follows. "If I had to recount the story of my life ever since I was born, it would be necessary, ladies, to take up a large part of yours: I wish only to tell you an adventure that happened to me with a very beautiful woman three or four years ago: I was already quite old; but Cupid has no respect for old age; on the contrary, he often enjoys making old people ridiculous. I was good friends with a lady who was very intelligent, who had a taste for philosophy: I myself played the philosopher; I was severe in criticizing even very young lovers: in short, I do not know how people could tolerate me. This lady, whom I shall call Madame de Fercy, became friendly with another lady who was named Madame de Rantal: this latter lady was not a philosopher: nature had bestowed many of its gifts upon her; she was young, agreeable, gracious, witty; her reason and her reflections took the place of philosophy in her; she often made fun of our idle disputes; and when Madame de Fercy wanted to engage her in reading Descartes and participating in our arguments, she would say: 'When I have seen you agree on something, not only will I read Descartes, but I will no longer read anything else; but as I see that you fail to reconcile your opinions after practically having come to blows, and since each person gives his/her own meaning to things that ought to be certain, you will allow me to restrict myself to my natural philosophy and not to waste my time and lungs on you people.' 'Now there is a fine philosophy!' replied Madame de Fercy; what benefit does it have?' 'I am going to tell you,' replied Madame de Rantal; 'first of all, never do I let myself get my hopes up to the point of being very angry when the things I plan do not succeed; I do not receive good and bad fortune with precisely the same composure; for I believe that this is linked more to lack of sensitivity than to philosophy; but good things do not cause me great transports of joy, and bad ones rarely have the power to grieve me to a great degree: I enjoy present good fortune, without wishing to penetrate a future that is always dark and uncertain; I content myself with a moderately good income, although I believe I deserve a greater one, and although I know perfectly well that I would not make a bad use of it: I ask of my friends only those things that I would do for them, and I even satisfy myself with much less: in short, of all the branches of philosophy I accept only ethics, but only the way I find it in my head and in my heart without the assistance of study: when I read, I prefer to learn facts that amuse me, rather than bore myself with abstract books, which would not make me wiser or more agreeable in company, and which contain knowledge that is quite uncertain.' 'There you have a perfect woman,' Madame de Fercy would then say as she mocked her friend: we would argue with her constantly; she would laugh about it, and we did not persuade her. During all these conversations, I felt the severity that I had acquired from age and study diminish within me. I found much intelligence in Madame de Rantal; her appearance was attractive: she had no thought of pleasing me; but a certain charming politeness with which nature had endowed her flattered my heart with some hope, and I felt myself in love, but in love like an Amadis.[105] Even before I could think of guarding myself against it, Madame de Fercy made me aware of it: at first I refused to admit it; but the extra care I was seen to take with my appearance, and the desire I had to please Madame de Rantal, revealed my feelings enough that my admission was not needed. I began to pay court to her with a little party that I gave for her; it was so lavish that Madame de Fercy could no longer doubt my passion. It was at the time when the jonquils and other spring flowers begin to bloom; my rooms were strewn all over with them: there

---

105. Hero of the best-selling fifteenth-century Spanish chivalric romance *Amadis of Gaul* by Garci Rodríguez de Montalvo. Amadis is the paragon of the devoted romantic hero, unfailingly faithful and blindly submissive to his beloved's every whim. The novel's popularity was enhanced by Lully and Quinault's 1684 opera of the same name.

was a large meal; a very pleasant concert followed it, and next I gave them a host of small entertainments that seemed quite amusing to them. Madame de Fercy, who is very good-humored and who did not want to claim any of the responsibility, always called her friend the Queen of the Party. A short time afterward, I arranged for a group of people to go spend four days in a marvelous house where I could do the honors; we left in the most beautiful month of the year, that is, the month of June; Madame de Rantal; Madame de Fercy; the Chevalier de Fercy her brother-in-law, who is young, very good looking and who has an excess of good qualities; a philosopher who did not leave Madame de Fercy's side; one of her female friends; and a man of my acquaintance who sings very well and who is very agreeable in conversation, especially at table. During our stay in this beautiful place I provided them with all the pleasures I could imagine. I come from a more gallant era than the current one. Nothing was forgotten to amuse an ungrateful woman who was starting to drive me to despair; abundance and refinement were the rule in our meals. I had brought along excellent musicians. There were concerts. We held lotteries in which all the tickets were black: the presents were not substantial; but there were pretty items in each prize drawing. We spent an afternoon on a ravishing little island constructed in the middle of a very large ornamental lake: this island is outfitted with freestones; four little towers are at the four corners; they each form a small room, one of which is a library with carefully selected, enjoyable books; the second has two black marble basins for baths; the third is filled with beautiful portraits, and the last is an aviary filled with birds that are pleasing to the sight and which, by their singing, make the air resound with a pleasing harmony: the middle of the island is occupied by a pavilion that forms a small and fully complete apartment; it is elegantly furnished; everything there inspires love; and the windows of this apartment look out over four different flower beds or grass plots. Madame de Rantal felt so happy in this place, to the beauty of which my description fails to do justice, that she admitted never having seen anything to equal it. I believed that this made her favorably disposed, and I asked her whether one might hope to be taken seriously if one declared one's feelings for her on this enchanted island. 'Oh no!' she replied; 'at least that would depend on the person. There are some individuals whom one would enjoy hearing even in a deserted area, and all the more so in a place as charming as this.' This remark, which of course she made by chance, did not fail to flatter my hopes. The next day, I had the carriage harnessed in order to drive the ladies into the park, which is one of the most beautiful in the kingdom; and as daylight was waning, I had us take the road back into the gardens. I ordered the carriage to stop at the foot of the waterfalls; and seeing that people were going their separate ways, I led Madame de Rantal toward a grotto whose waters are perpetually in motion, and which, being close to a wood, is at the proper distance to hear the nightingales; she made no difficulty about entering; she found the interior and location of the grotto very agreeable. I did not want to lose a moment that I deemed so favorable; I threw myself at her feet; I told her some very touching things; I made her a vivid depiction of my torments and of my passion: she laughed wholeheartedly, and was not answering, when she heard these words addressed to her by a very beautiful voice.

> *Shun love, young beauty, and beware:*
> *When you hear complaints of torment from young swains,*
> *Oft what they dare say of their pains*
> *Greatly distorts truth, trait most fair;*
> *But when men of a solid age*
> *Follow blind Cupid's tutelage,*
> *They're true and faithful beyond compare.*

'You have spoiled everything,' she told me, laughing, when the singing was finished; 'you should have limited yourself to the declaration that you made to me: this looks so prepared that it fails to be moving.' Madame de Rantal's tone of voice was so mocking, and I was so certain that I saw in her eyes a desire to leave the grotto, that anger overcame me and I said a thousand outrageous things. You can easily judge, ladies, that I had commissioned this text and that I had stationed one of my singers in this place with precise orders to sing it when I arrived with Madame de Rantal: my efforts did not work out as planned, as you see. I was in a very foul mood for the rest of the evening. Madame de Fercy noticed this, she teased me about it; but that was no longer what was occupying my thoughts. The Chevalier de Fercy was looking at Madame de Rantal, and she kept returning his glances; between them was emerging a love that was at first a big mystery, and I believe I noted that one of their reasons for being so discreet was the presence of Madame de Fercy, who was not indifferent toward her brother-in-law. This discovery drove me to despair, and I returned home to Paris having gained jealousy and having lost hope. Nothing makes a man more unhappy; however, I decided to try again from the financial angle. Madame de Rantal was not rich; she loved luxury. I believed that this path would garner me more advantage; but I was dealing with a woman who had a passion and who was so little attached to selfish interests that she would have given the crown of the universe in order to see her lover with more freedom. I sought to be avenged; I revealed the secret of their love to Madame de Fercy, who already had strong suspicions: she is more dangerous than the ordinary woman when she is angered: her rival had to suffer; her brother-in-law was tormented: these setbacks increased the passion of these two lovers, and the jealous Fercy and myself discovered only the secret for making ourselves very unhappy, while making others very miserable.

You see, ladies, that I am not vainglorious, and that I freely admit the harshness with which I was treated."

"You should not have told such a story," I told him when I saw that he had finished; "nothing determines our behavior so well as examples; and a woman who would have considered it an honor to have made you her slave, if you had been fortunate in the episode you described, would perhaps be ashamed to remedy your misfortune." The duke was sensitive to the cruelty of this jesting: I saw that, and I had the time to regret it. He was no longer able to restrain his agitation; starting on that very day he would never leave my side, and Brésy was unable to speak to me even for a moment. He noticed the next day that we found his presence very annoying: he needed someone to whom to pour out the feelings of his heart; it was to Madame d'Orselis that he confided his sorrows. Just a day or two earlier she had had a falling out with the chevalier. A combination of her natural inclinations and her idleness made her compose songs attacking Madame d'Arcire and me. There were also some songs attacking herself in order to deflect suspicion from her. The Duke de . . . received these as a packet arriving from Paris. We were so badly treated in those poems, and our stay at the count's house was portrayed in such a dreadful light that the marquise wanted to leave the very next day: but I maintained to her that we should not leave one moment early; that it was more prudent to scorn the poet than to appear to fear him. "Besides," I added, "I have no doubt that this is a trick played by our elderly duke and by Madame d'Orselis: they would be only too content to chase us away from a place where we were scheduled to remain only a short time longer. Believe me, madam, let us stay and let us get back at them."

Indeed, we in our turn received songs in which the duke was treated as he deserved and in which the beautiful and malicious Orselis was not spared. Selincourt was too much in love with Madame d'Arcire for him not to abandon his uncle to us. The marquis, who was not patient by nature, no longer troubled himself with the old duke's constant attentions; and he did not fail to come and interrupt the duke as he came to speak to me. One evening, when everything was rather calm between us, we engaged Madame d'Arcire to tell us something of her adventures: for, we told her, we need to know something about the people with whom we are dealing when we are living together. She consented and began the narrative that we asked her for in this manner.

"I was very young when Monsieur d'Arcire began to show romantic interest in me. At first he looked upon me as a suitable match; but soon after he truly came to love me and wished to obtain me from my heart, rather than from my parents. He was very intelligent, and his figure was noble and agreeable. He had a certain elegance that is derived from refined company and is not found among lower-class people. I found him extremely pleasing; I did not want to show any of my feelings: but the experience he had acquired from being ten years older than me did not allow him to be mistaken. He discerned with a perceptible pleasure the agitations of a young heart that was unable to resist him. His plan was to become my husband; he neglected no step to prove his love to me respectfully and to oblige me to return his affection. My mother, who saw his attachment, would not have been displeased if he had declared his intentions; but he had not yet spoken of them, and I often received severe reprimands for allowing him to whisper a few words to me. I loved him, I admit that: he, however, was content to be aware of that truth, and was able to forego my speaking it. I did not have the boldness to reply to him. A whole year went by with this silence on my part. Gradually my contact with society made me more assured. I spoke several words to him, which raised his happiness to its highest level. He had an ingratiating spirit, against which it was not possible to defend oneself. My mother vainly tried to forbid his visits. He spoke to her in such a way that, without saying anything specific, he left her with hopes that were sufficient for her. When he was absent, he would write to her: it was even permitted to him to write to me too, provided that it was in the same packet of letters. His manner of writing was playful, and he had a lot of imagination.

We went away for a trip to an estate belonging to my family, in a beautiful province. Everyone was eager to entertain us, and we attended a party at the home of one of my relatives that lasted a week. There were often hunting expeditions; we danced; there was excellent food; we played various games; there was total freedom there, and the company was quite good, although it was numerous. One day, as we were leaving the dinner table, a packet of letters from Monsieur d'Arcire was brought to my mother. He was a hundred leagues away, kept there by his official functions. He was sending us word in a delicate manner how sad he was not to be able to be where we were. It was his native region, no one would have found it strange if he had been seen there. I got a separate letter, which I took after it had been read aloud. And since he wrote well and one reads more than once what comes from people one loves, I went into the garden with one of my girlfriends with whom I reread it. While I was engrossed in this, I heard a noise. Shortly after, I heard my name uttered by a woman who was running toward us with a man whom I soon recognized as Monsieur d'Arcire. Anyone who has never experienced such a surprise has never felt true pleasure! Just imagine a young person, whose heart was tender, charmed by reading a mere letter, distressed by an absence that delayed the joy of seeing her lover, and who at that very instant saw him before her eyes. Again, I do not know whether your imagination can furnish you ideas that come close to what I felt in that delightful moment. I blushed, I turned pale, I became embarrassed, I lowered my eyes, and I did not say a word.

I do not believe I am violating the rules of decorum by admitting the feelings that I had for a man whom I married; but you must hear the rest. It is indeed true that this posthaste trip, as rushed as that of a messenger, flattered my vanity and my heart. However, I retained so much self-control that, amid such a large company, where people had total freedom, despite the pleasure I was feeling and the extreme pleasure that Monsieur d'Arcire had in speaking to me, I avoided a private conversation with him so carefully that in the four days that he spent in our house with us, he did not have the satisfaction of speaking a word to me in private. My reasons for maintaining that behavior were that a man who arrived so hastily in a place where he barely knew the master constituted an effect of keen passion, of which I could not help appearing the object, since he was well acquainted with no one except my mother and me. You see that I was a sensible person and that my reasoning was quite sound. People guessed his secret all the same; but at least I could not be accused of being in complicity with him.

Monsieur d'Arcire made use of another language that was permitted to him. He gazed at me ardently; and as he sought in my eyes the cause of my severe behavior, I do not know whether he guessed it, or whether a certain gentle joy that he saw shine forth in my actions was what made him conjecture that he was not badly thought of by me. But after making many useless attempts, he contented himself with telling me pleasing things during the various games that we were playing for amusement. He proposed proverb plays. It was at that time that I learned to perform them. He was a marvelous actor; and he directed the people he acted with so well that I always had things to keep myself occupied. I cannot pass over in silence a story that he recounted to us one day, when everyone was obliged to tell one. It is extraordinary enough to deserve telling; and a confirmed fact that has come to the knowledge of many people. Here is how he told it.

'I have just come back from deep in the Bourbonnais region, as you know, ladies: Comminge came through that area while I was there; it is from that very person that I heard the story I am going to tell you.[106] He was traveling in the Berry region and often took back roads. One evening he arrived at a poor-quality inn where he was known and where the own-

---

106. Presumably Louis de Comminges (1654–1732), a respected military officer who won the esteem of the king but led a dissolute life. The ancient noble Comminges family had contributed numerous distinguished military officers and diplomats over the centuries.

ers would have gladly received him; but the circumstances were against it, and the small amount of lodging room in the house was occupied by people whom the owners did not dare force out; there remained only a low-roofed room, exceptionally uncomfortable, with a tiny room to the side, where they set up a wretched bed for a friend of Comminge who was traveling with him. They took their supper together; it was cold, a big fire was lit; and since they wanted to depart early in the morning, Comminge's personal valet put a candle in the chimney of his room: that, ladies, is precisely how all ghost stories begin.

The two friends fell asleep just as if they had been lying on superb mattresses. Hardly had Comminge begun to doze off than his friend screamed at the top of his lungs: "Comminge, Comminge, something is strangling me!" Comminge, who was in his first slumber, answered a few words and fell back to sleep immediately; however, the sleep was not so deep that anxiety did not wake him up a short time afterward. He called his friend; he got no answer. He went to get a candle and entered the tiny room where his unfortunate friend was. But what astonishment he felt when he found the friend motionless and without a pulse, and grabbed around the neck by a dead man completely covered with chains! The spectacle was horrifying. Comminge made loud cries to call for help. The master of the house came, wearing his nightcap and holding a lamp from the kitchen in his hand, and he was very surprised when he saw this mishap. They sent off for medical help for Comminge's friend before getting to the bottom of the mystery. They ran to wake up the village barber in order to bleed him. They brought in a mirror to see whether he was still breathing. They confirmed that he was not dead. With difficulty, they pulled away the dead man who was gripping him very firmly: and once they saw that the remedies were having their effect, Comminge learned from the host that this was his valet from the stable, who for the past few days had suffered from a brain fever that made him so out of control; that they had chained him in the stable; that apparently he had broken his chains; that he had passed through a little door that connected that stable to the tiny room; and that he had come to expire upon the bed of the unfortunate traveler. That, ladies, is the truth of that story, which is, in my opinion, far more terrifying than anything that is told about ghosts: for this is real; deception of the senses plays no part in it. Comminge's friend was cured in a few days, he admitted that he had never had so great a fright. And as for me, I truly believe that nothing could be so scary as the moments that preceded his fainting.'

That is how Monsieur d'Arcire finished his little narrative. All the women had nearly died of fear and found themselves very relieved that it was a dead man rather than a ghost. It remains for me to tell you that we stayed one more day in the place where we were, and that afterward we traveled back to my mother's estate: Monsieur d'Arcire had permission to follow us there: he then got his revenge to some extent; for since we were no longer so closely observed, I took the liberty of listening to him and of responding to him. He went away to see his family, who were one day's journey from us. My mother also had in that general area a relative whom she went to see; this relative was unattractive and she was past her youth: she had a very lively, and therefore very unfortunate, passion for Monsieur d'Arcire; I believe, however, that in periods of idleness he had dallied with her, he loved to see himself loved; but the way he treated her in front of me was not appealing; his manner and his words were always sarcastic: she felt despair deep within her heart; but she is intelligent and knows how to hide her feelings: she would speak to my mother in favor of Monsieur d'Arcire, who had not, however, confided his plans to her; but she wanted to get into my mother's good graces and to indicate discreetly to Monsieur d'Arcire that she loved him. Later, in order to take revenge on me, she invented entire fictional plots, of which she made me the heroine; they were executed under the guise of compassion for a charming girl from among her relatives who was on the verge of ruining herself with this conduct: at the same time she exhorted Monsieur d'Arcire to marry me, in order, she said, to rescue me from so dangerous a situation. At first she had the power to make him feel the dagger that she was plunging into him so artfully; but he insisted on getting to the bottom of these accusations and found them so false that one day, as she was still trying to give him bad impressions about me, and accompanying these with pleas to exhort him to marry me, he told her, 'Yes, madam, I will marry your charming relative; but it will not be to restore this reputation that you are constantly tearing to pieces; it will be to crown the virtue of a girl who is above reproach.' A bolt of lightning cannot compare to the effect that such terrifying words had upon her; she was totally disconcerted by them; and despite this pernicious woman, who was dying of love and fury, I married Monsieur d'Arcire a short time after I had returned to Paris, and we spent some very happy days together: it is true that since a very cruel death tore him away from me, I was unable to prevent myself from letting this ill-treated lover know, when an opportunity presented itself, that I was informed of everything that had happened between her and Monsieur d'Arcire. This was no slight annoyance to her; for she passes herself off as a devout person, and nothing could displease her more than whatever persuaded me that she was just the opposite." Madame d'Arcire finished her narrative, and we all thanked her for the pleasure that she had given us. There was no one who was displeased apart from the count, whose tenderness, or rather bizarre humor, could not be reconciled with the knowledge that his predecessor had been so perfectly loved; but that was a cloud that soon dissipated.

The following day, Madame de Richardin came to return our call: she was dressed completely in pink; her husband wore a military jacket made of buffalo leather and a green plume, he escorted her gravely like a squire; the little lackey in red carried her train up to the middle of the gallery where we were at that moment, and her tall daughter had on a simple brown grisette.[107] We received Madame de Richardin as if she were the Queen of Cythera;[108] Brésy threw himself at her feet and assured her that he had not felt healthy for a moment since he had come back from her house, and that was what had prevented him from fulfilling his duty toward her. Since Brésy had not replied to Madame de Richardin with all the tenderness that she had imagined he was supposed to have for her, she began again several times to speak to him in that same tone of voice; but noticing that, far from constraining himself, he would answer her with a mocking smile, she said, rising abruptly: "Let us get out of here, the people here do not know how to receive persons like me." Monsieur de Richardin, whom Selincourt had engaged in conversation in order to do the honors of his house, was very surprised at his wife's prompt departure; but he made ready to obey her. Meanwhile, Selincourt, who correctly judged that Madame de Richardin's bad mood was caused by

107. Short garment made of inexpensive gray cloth.
108. See note 4 in the translation, p. 23.

Brésy's indifference, approached her and proposed to her that they take a light meal before departing. Madame de Richardin refused with an angry look; and followed by her tall daughter and her husband, she left with great haste. As soon as old Richardin was in her carriage, a remnant of hope, or a regret for the outrageous manner of her departure, caused her to pretend to be ill. "Have them stop," she said to her husband, "I am feeling unwell." The poor man did not dare to oppose someone whose will was accustomed to overriding his own; he alighted from the carriage with his little wife; and, supporting her on one side and his daughter on the other, they came back to join us. The spectacle struck us as un-usual, and the sight of the little Richardin in a faint, or rather play-acting, caused us to burst out laughing so hard that the count was obliged to silence us in order to fulfill his duty as master of the house.

The ailing woman was placed on a sofa; her husband and her daugh-ter acted distressed: this inconvenienced Madame de Richardin; she had her plans, and she told them in a tone of voice harsh enough to make them tremble: "Get out of here! Leave me in peace; I am not in a state to return to my château to lie down." We were very surprised by this resolution; the matter concerned everyone, each of us imagined a means for preventing her from carrying it out: "Madame de Richardin does me great honor," said Selincourt, "but I am afraid that I lack countless things here that are required for an illness as pressing as hers." "Our female servants are so clumsy," added the marquise, "that a person as delicate as Madame might perhaps find herself poorly attended." "That is not the real difficulty," Brésy continued; "I would gladly serve as her personal valet; but," he added, lowering his voice, "where will you put her? You know about the strange noises in the only apartment that would be worthy of her." "As for me," said Selincourt, capitalizing perfectly on the marquis's train of thought, "one night, I insisted on being coura-geous, but I believed that all the devils were let loose in that apartment. However great the advantage that would be conferred upon us by having Madame de Richardin here, I have a consideration for her that prevents me from wishing to acquire that pleasure at the expense of the frights that she might experience." This conversation was carried on in a dis-creet tone of voice that was still fully audible and had the effect that we were wishing for. "Ghosts!" exclaimed Madame de Richardin. "Ghosts!"

she repeated, crying out at the top of her lungs. "Have someone call Monsieur de Richardin. I must leave immediately." Then, forgetting her illness, she began to run toward the courtyard: fortunately, her husband and her daughter were in no hurry to depart and were enjoying themselves over the light meal. Since each of us was delighted by this woman's fear, we ran after her to lead her back inside. The ghosts had upset her wits to such an extent that she refused to say a proper farewell and she jumped, with great agility, into her carriage.

As soon as we had gotten rid of her, we reviewed all her faults: her pride, her presumption, her ridiculous airs, her passions; but we concluded that nothing in her was as highly developed as fear, because that emotion had made her forget her pretended illness or disturb her amorous intentions. "Did you see," said the marquise, "the fright all over her face when the marquis first mentioned ghosts? If she had actually seen the ghosts that he was speaking of, what more extreme reaction could she have had?" "Indeed," Brésy then said, "the mere idea dealt her a mortal blow." "Upon my word," said Chanteuil, "if Madame de M . . . had not displayed more courage than she did, B . . . would never have found happiness." "What," said the marquise, "you know a ghost story, and you have hidden it from us until now?" "I thought," rejoined Chanteuil, "that everyone knew about this adventure." The count added that at least there were few people who did not know of it. "As for me," replied Madame d'Arcire, "I have never heard it spoken of." Madame d'Orselis said the same thing. I admitted that I knew it perfectly; and we obliged the chevalier to tell us the story. Here is how he discharged that obligation.

"M . . . was a brave man who had done distinguished service in an illustrious army unit; B . . . was his friend; but he fell in love with his wife and made him jealous: M . . . , however, did not stop seeing him, in order not to create a public scandal; but on his deathbed he begged Madame de M . . . never to allow his friend to occupy his place. Madame de M . . . promised nothing; her tears choked her, and her plan was not to commit herself to a matter in which the heart ought to be in control. Thus, her husband died without being sure of how things stood. B . . . , who was greatly in love and who was far from being hated by her, soon consoled the charming widow: they promised each other that they would wed at the end of the mourning period and during that year they enjoyed the first charms of hope. When the time for their happiness had arrived, they resolved to get married without fuss and without any witnesses other than their love and a few servants. The time for the ceremony was set for midnight, and these lovers, sitting at their fireside, were telling each other the sorts of things that are never boring, when one of Madame de M . . .'s daughters, who was only seven years old and who was near them, cried out: 'Ah, there is my father!' Madame de M . . . turned her head and saw him all too clearly. B . . . , a man of good sense and of fearlessness that had been displayed in the greatest dangers, looked and saw the same thing. He got up and drew his sword and advanced toward the phantom. The phantom parried his thrusts with its two hands, without seeming troubled at this pursuit, which could not do it any harm. B . . . interrogated it; the ghost remained silent and very subtly glided behind a window curtain. B . . . ran over to it, lifted the curtain, and found nothing more. I do not know whether he felt any pang of fear; but his passion would have made him overcome any obstacle. He vainly urged Madame de M . . . to make him a happy man, despite the apparition. She was dying of fear; her husband's final words struck her at that moment with such force that, without explaining her intention, she postponed her marriage with B . . . , even though they were expected at the church. This adventure was made public. B . . . , who believed, with good reason, that it is just as ridiculous to deny a fact as to have a wild imagination, admitted to all his friends that this story was true; and it was only with time that Madame de M . . . made up her mind to remarry. This union did not fail to be happy later on. People more easily frightened or less in love would have obeyed the tacit order of M . . .'s spirit and would have deprived themselves of much contentment."

This story scared us a bit; the characters are reasonable people, and it would be hard to believe them capable of attacks of frailty that furnish delusions. The marquise and Madame d'Orselis reasoned at length over this story, which is doubtless very surprising; and the count, the marquis and the chevalier assured us that there was not one of them who would not agree to undergo such an adventure in order to obtain a beautiful woman with whom they were in love.

The day following the departure of old Richardin, having spent the whole day without tiresome people, I took this occasion to ask Brésy for the narrative that he had promised us of some of his adventures. Here is how he acquitted himself of that task.

"It happened three years ago, ladies, that, deceived by a lovers' quarrel and believing that I was no longer in love, I found myself at the opera next to a pretty woman whom I did not know; she appeared to me so brilliant by the sparkle of her wit that the two ladies who were two paces away from her, though perfect beauties, attracted my gaze only in order to deflect it, with greater pleasure, toward a person who was merely pleasant looking, but who pleased me enormously; I believe I can say that I did not displease her: she was receptive to the praises that I gave her. One of my friends wanted to drag me away as soon as the opera was over; I told him to leave by himself; I waited for the crowd to disperse, and I resolved to get introduced to Madame d'Arbure; that was her name. I found her the next day at the theater: I spoke to her longer than the previous day: her eyes were sparkling with a lively and engaging fire; I henceforth spoke of nothing but her; I gave her all the praises that one gives to persons whom one loves: that was to her liking, she was grateful to me for it; she no longer saw me without an agitation that proved her modesty and her feelings. One day I put myself in her path to speak to her as she was leaving the opera; but a man gave her his arm. I was unable to go up to her, and I noticed with a palpable pleasure that she made a point of looking at me. I had known for a long time that I had a rival: those are not always the ones who are most to be feared; but this one was dangerous because of the regard she had for him. I wrote a note, which I gave to be delivered by one of my servants, as intelligent a man as there ever was with these sorts of matters, and whom I made use of whenever I got mixed up in love affairs. 'Don't go making a mistake,' I told him upon giving him my note, 'place it in the hands of no one but Madame d'Arbure.' 'For that you must believe I am an idiot,' he replied to me. 'Oh, sir, I know perfectly well whom I must beware of!' 'And who is that?' I rejoined, to see how far his knowledge of the matter went. He named my rival precisely. 'All right, go on,' I told him, 'you know more than enough not to do your duty.' Indeed, he consistently refused to give my note to a chambermaid who did not want to enter her mistress's room because she was in bed. His persistence finally gained him entry; he presented her with the letter like a man of great experience: and having told her my name, he saw that Madame d'Arbure blushed while reading it. The letter contained language approximately as follows:

> If the effects that you have produced upon my heart have caused some agitation in yours, I would not trade my felicity against that of the gods. Shall I tell you, madam, everything that I am thinking? I flatter myself that I can aspire to that glory. Do not be annoyed with me for a vanity that has its origin in my desires, and, if possible, confirm to me what I thought I saw in your beautiful eyes.

The charming Madame d'Arbure answered me in these terms:

> Your letter does not contain a certain natural quality that I would like to see in it: the truth is that you have quarreled with a mistress who is unworthy of you; but by whom you continue to be enchanted. I am perhaps not the one destined to break this charm: it is undoubtedly in order to get over your sorrow that you are attempting to disturb my heart, and that heart has in fact been troubled, despite my second thoughts.

She was right, ladies: I was in love with the most coquettish woman there ever was; I fully recognized that later: but at that moment I looked upon her as a goddess: I only wished to annoy her through a seeming liaison with a pretty woman: and if Madame d'Arbure pleased me more than another woman, she was very far from making me forget my faithless one. I was still quite content with her answer: I had her followed that afternoon: I learned that she was in a house where I was a frequent guest. I did not fail to make an appearance there: she had no doubt that this visit was meant for her: I hardly concealed that fact from her. While the mistress of the house was speaking to other people, I had the liberty to inform her in a few words of the attention with which I was seeking her out. Later we remained alone with the lady whom she had come to see: the conversation had to involve all three of us: it was so lively and so charming on the part of my new beloved, that at that moment I believed myself to be very much in love and very fortunate. It was late when we separated: I deposited her in her carriage; I asked her to be present the next day at the opera; she promised me to do so, and I had the pleasure of seeing the next day that she kept her word to me.

The following day I went to Madame d'Arbure's house at four in the afternoon: she was alone; a servant went off to announce me; she came out to meet me. 'Why have you come?' she asked me. 'Did I not tell you yesterday not to come?' 'It is true,' I told her with an air of assurance, 'that you forbade me to do so: but I believed that I was sufficiently unhappy because of that prohibition, without increasing my sorrow by obeying you precisely.' My answer was quite impertinent, I admit; but Madame d'Arbure made no comment on it. 'What shall I say,' she replied, 'if someone finds you here? I will be very embarrassed: you have never been seen here; nobody has brought you here; people will make censorious remarks about this visit.' 'Very well,' I told her; 'nothing is easier than to help you out of this difficulty. I will send my carriage away: then you must order your door to be closed to everyone.' The expedient seemed wondrously prudent: we made use of it, and I remained until evening with the charming Madame d'Arbure. One cannot get bored with her: she has the most brilliant imagination and the most lively expressions possible. She even has an appearance of modesty that adds enormously to the tender things she says; and one always believes that she is experiencing her very first passion.

I visited her this way over several days: but the fatal star guiding my destiny led me to a place where my other beloved renewed her hold on me so fully that, not only did I have the weakness to make up with her, I further had the injustice of putting in her power the secret of a woman a hundred times more likable than she was. I admit my faults to you, ladies: I visited Madame d'Arbure less often: she suspected the cause of this change of affection: she complained of it tenderly, but uselessly. She asked me to return her letters: I gave them back to her at once. There already you have an example of fickleness in my past. Here is another one that is just as bad. It was reported to Madame d'Arbure that I had been indiscreet: she was even told more than what I had really said. She insisted on an explanation from me: I gave her one, more or less convincing. On that occasion she seemed to me more attractive than ever: I wished to appease her; I realize how stupendous a power I had over her heart: there has never been another one like it; but she is proud, and I accomplished nothing. A short time later I left for the army. My mistress, who had heard it said that those who are absent are always in the wrong, quarreled with me before my departure. I left Paris, persuaded that I had to forget that unfaithful woman. The idleness during the course of the military campaign, which was great that year, made me resolve to write to Madame d'Arbure. I did so at first like a man who sincerely repents for his conduct: she answered me like a woman who was granting my pardon. I next wrote in the style of a friend: she fully went along with my proposal that she should be my friend. Her letters were charming: in them friendship was depicted in terms that could have made Cupid himself jealous. I was angry with that woman who had left me: I believed in good faith that I felt passion for Madame d'Arbure. My letters began to become more tender. She begged me not to interfere with the resolution that she had made, to look upon me only as her friend. She vividly reminded me of the way I had treated her; and finished by telling me that my friendship would touch her more than the passion of another man; and that my love, even if it gave her much pleasure, would be followed by excessively cruel pain. Those sorts of things do not discourage someone: there was a certain grace in all her words that passed right into my heart. I can even show you one of her letters that remained in my possession, and which she wrote to me during that period." With those words, the marquis took that letter out of his pocket and read the following text:

What have I done to you, that you are still after my heart, without feeling yourself worthy to possess it, or capable of keeping it for long? Do you not know to what point your heart is necessary to my happiness? Do you require yet another mark of my weakness in order to complete your triumph? I have loved you only too much: I displayed it to you quite warmly; you sacrificed me to another. All my hatred was directed toward my rival: all my tenderness remained for you; I admit to you, to my shame, that I have never for a moment stopped loving you: but what do you wish to do with this admission? You will make it an offering, perhaps, to this new fairy, who holds you in her spell. Ah, I would rather die than consent to a renewed relationship that will bring down a new torment upon me! I do not wish to hear anything more of you; forget me, down to my name. But what will I gain by depriving myself of the sweetness of seeing you and receiving news of you? What does it matter how I lose my life? Will I not die if I do not see you again?

We all found this letter very tender. The marquis resumed his narrative as follows: "I was touched by this letter; I sent her so many declarations; I assured her so strongly of a constant love; I depicted so well to her the pleasure that I would have to see her again, that she was no longer able to resist a man for whom she felt an unconquerable affection. We wrote to each other every day during the rest of the campaign. I sent her my portrait; she sent me hers:[109] I felt with rapture the approaching time of my return; I went to her home two hours after my arrival. Her rapture and mine are beyond description. For two weeks I was the happiest man in the universe. She abandoned everyone else in the world in order to see only me. My happiness was too charming to last: I learned that my other beloved was occupied with two or three young men. I went to her home one afternoon with the sole intention of astonishing her suitors by the appearance of a suitor who was once loved. But I do not know how Cupid got involved: my rivals yielded their place to me: the faithless woman asked my pardon; I made up with her, and once again I left the tender, the witty, the divine Madame d'Arbure. I wrote her an eloquent text to justify the bizarre inclination that I felt for a woman whom I admitted to be much inferior to her. Madame d'Arbure felt the worst that amorous resentment can inspire: but because of her tenderness for me and her natural gentleness, she wrote to me only something that a perceptible grief is capable of inspiring in the most charming of lovers. I condemn myself, I did so even at the time; but I was indeed bewitched, and no one had the power to end the relationship. Since then I have received twenty tokens of passion from Madame d'Arbure: she did everything she could to conserve my affection for herself; but whether it was out of embarrassment or whimsy, I did not respond to them. Since then I have broken up definitively with her rival; I have had dalliances with women, without feeling passion; one must agree that such a situation is not too agreeable. To conclude, I have gotten over the follies of my youth, and I find myself

109. See note 57 in the translation, p. 60.

only too capable of a manner of loving which is a hundred times more touching and with which, until the present, I was unfamiliar."

The marquis thus finished his narrative; the examples of his fickleness caused me some pangs of sorrow; but I hid them with care. We commented upon Brésy's adventures: that evening Selincourt was in a charming mood; he proposed that we go to the opera the following day: he told us that he had already sent relay horses to three places along the route; we would come back the same day. The weather was marvelous and there was beautiful moonlight; we agreed that it would be an enjoyable folly. Madame d'Orselis, who sometimes prides herself on being strictly logical, pointed out that we were departing in a few days, and that this would be a hurried trip for no good reason. Madame d'Arcire and I protested against her severity; Chanteuil, who would come back to her from time to time in order to avoid the statute of limitations,[110] fought against her position: she gave in, and, without getting up earlier than usual, we departed, and we arrived a quarter of an hour before the opera began. At the performance we found many of our friends who believed we were back in town and who came to call on us the following day. Our servants, who had not been informed of this little trip, believed that our friends were dreaming when they told them that they had seen us. We left again after the opera, and with our relays, we arrived at the Selincourt estate before midnight. The next day we asked the count, as with the others, to tell us some of his adventures. He agreed to submit to this order: here is how he acquitted himself of it.

"Several years ago, ladies, while at Fontainebleau, I renewed acquaintance with a woman in whose house I had been several times when she was a girl, and whom I had lost sight of since. I found her more charming than ever; it seemed to me that she took pleasure in seeing me again. I contributed to entertaining her while she was at Fontainebleau; I escorted her to the theater; I took her for walks; my retinue was at her disposal; I whispered sweet nothings to her, to which she listened mysteriously. One of my friends who had failed with her did not refuse to do me a good turn because he needed me, and he knows that these are the services for which

110. According to the laws of gallantry, a suitor had a limited grace period in which to return to his beloved after a quarrel before losing her favor entirely.

one feels the most gratitude; she saw me so assiduous as a courtier waiting on the King (for you know, ladies, that I did not fail in any of my duties) that she was enormously grateful to me for what I was doing for her and for the time that I was giving her: especially when I missed the *coucher*[III] in order to spend a longer time with her, she congratulated herself for that, and that was her vulnerable spot. Finally, when she departed for one of her estates, I was already on quite close terms with her. I wrote to her; she wrote me back. I went to her home as soon as she was back in Paris: visits from other people seemed long to her, she had consideration only for me out of the throngs of people who saw her; I noticed in her a charming anxiety when someone else arrived during my visit; she constantly had her eyes on me, to see whether or not I was preparing to leave. I must admit that I was sometimes mischievous enough to take my leave of her, though I had no business to attend to elsewhere; it was on that type of occasion that her heart declared itself: she had, she would say, a word to tell me; that word was nothing, it was only to stop me from going. However, I did not yet have any genuine proofs of this tenderness that delighted me; I often complained to her about that, but I made no progress. One of her female friends, beautiful, attractive and extremely diverting, took it into her head to fancy me, while I was in the situation that I have just described to you. Cruelty would not suit me well; I responded quite favorably to this woman, although in fact I loved Madame de Sardise a hundred times better. I went to her rival's home several times; she found out about it; she nearly died of grief. She complained to me about it in a manner that made me repent of my infidelity. 'That, madam, is what happens,' I told her, 'when you make an unfortunate lover languish too long; he takes anyone he finds on his path; but if I were sure of your heart, I would abandon everyone else in the world.' Madame de Sardise truly loved me: I now had reason to be content with her: she made me happy with graceful touches that added enormously to it; she has an adorable modesty, and she showed perfect attention to everything that could prove her tenderness to me. I believed myself beyond the reach of fortune; I was charmed to have made this illustrious conquest: she

---

III. A court ceremony in which a group of privileged courtiers were invited to watch the king change into his bedclothes and retire for the night.

knew the value of what she was doing for me, and judging too favorably of my gratitude, she had not wished to stop seeing Madame d'Ardane, for fear of appearing jealous on her account. I had not gone to see the latter lady for a long time; she seized her occasion to reproach me for it while her friend was speaking to someone else; I promised her to go there the following day. She was very far from having Madame de Sardise's delicacy: she was even comfortable competing with her, provided that she thought that she had an equal share in my heart. But Madame de Sardise had forbidden me to go to her home. That was the price that she had attached to her favors. This charming woman, after making some visits, came by her rival's house to take her to the Tuileries. My carriage was at the door: she saw that with a throbbing heart and a despair that cannot be expressed. One of her servants had already left to find out whether the rival wished to come downstairs. Indeed, we had to come downstairs, the secret was discovered, there was no means of retreating. Madame d'Ardane did not lose countenance as she entered the carriage. As for me, I was as pale as a criminal, and I did not dare to say more than one word to Madame de Sardise. I believe that their conversation was chilly while they were alone. I soon went to join them. One of my male friends kept Madame d'Ardane amused while I attempted to appease Madame de Sardise. 'Why are you treating me this way?' I asked her, seeing that she was not speaking to me. 'What have I done to you?' 'What you have done to me!' she retorted, her eyes wet with tears. 'What you have done to me!' she repeated. 'Do I need to tell you? What has it not cost me to attach you to me? You have led me down the path of jealousy into a labyrinth from which I can no longer escape. I love you more than my life: I have done everything to prove it to you. All I ask from you in return is to stop seeing that woman: I find you at her house a short time after, and perhaps you go there every day. And even if you went there today for the first time,' she added, 'that is more than enough cause for me to abandon you to your faithlessness and to never see you again in my life.' 'No, madam, no,' I said to her, 'you will not treat me that way. I was in the wrong: but this woman asks me to go see her; she shows me kindness, where would the politeness be in refusing her request?' 'Politeness,' she hastily replied; 'that trait is well placed. Ah, Selincourt, it is better to be uncivil than inconstant!' I begged, I pleaded, without being able to obtain my pardon that day: but soon after I obtained it, on the condition of never going to see Madame d'Ardane at her home. Madame de Sardise, who has integrity, did not believe that anyone could lack this quality with her, especially after the oaths that I swore to her. And since that woman amused her, and since she wished to attempt to hide our affection from her, she often included her in our outings. One of her male friends wished to give a party for her at Saint-Cloud: she proposed that I attend. My court duties required my presence at Versailles at the time of the trip: I got her to see reason on this point. It is true that, knowing that Madame d'Ardane was supposed to be part of that gathering, I went over to her house for a moment. She was being fitted for a gown: there were several waiting women around her. She whispered to me that, since I was not going to Saint-Cloud, she would dispense with going there, because it would be too boring. I remained so briefly at her home that I did not have the time to sit down; for I was afraid of being discovered. A moment after I had left, Madame de Sardise arrived and abruptly got out of her carriage in order to go up to Madame d'Ardane's apartments. The latter, who feared that her attendants would mention my name, rushed to meet her, not fully dressed, and complained of a headache that prevented her from joining the outing. Several days later, the proposal was made to go to a beautiful estate in the environs of Paris. In addition to these two ladies, there was one other lady and two men, who rarely left our side. One of the men, during the trip out there, gave us a very detailed account of a liaison that he was having with a very rich widow, and he admitted to us that she often had him followed, because she was very jealous. Upon arriving at the door of the place where we were going, he saw her carriage harnessed to six horses, which was arriving at almost the exact same time as we were. He let out a cry of astonishment and told us agitatedly that he was certainly discovered. We exhorted him to take courage, and we made our way inside in a direction where we thought we would be safe from attack. In that place we came to the edge of a fountain; and through a frightening bit of absent-mindedness, I told Madame d'Ardane that she was wearing the very gown that I had seen her try on several days before. Madame de Sardise, attentive to everything I said, heard this remark all too well, although the other lady quickly changed the subject. She looked at me in a manner that disconcerted me, and the three of us remained rather embarrassed. The others, who were not apprised of the state of things, attempted to restart the conversation; but soon the entire situation changed. A fair creature worthy of our attention suddenly appeared before us; the lover of our friend, in one of those sedan-chairs that was carried by men, the fat R . . . , who was in another sedan-chair, female servants behind, and several men who completed the entourage, composed together a genuine spectacle: for we were in a valley, and this magnificent display was processing above us on a terrace. The jealous widow, who was there only to seek her lover, had no sooner spotted him among us when she had her sedan-chair stopped in order to get down. 'Hurry to do your duty,' we told him; 'go and offer your arm to your Andromaque.'[112] That lady was dressed in precisely the same way with her long mourning attire. He ran to her; he flew to her; but he was poorly received. 'Go back,' she told him, 'deceitful man; go back to the side of Madame de Sardise: I only wanted to see you there with her, and I am now all too satisfied.' The lady's indiscretion and her fury did not permit her to lower her voice; on the contrary, she pronounced those terrifying words with a ringing voice; and supporting herself on the arms of one of her waiting women, she sought refuge in the thickest part of the forest, like a genuine heroine in distress; meanwhile, Madame de Sardise blushed. I believed at that moment that the widow was right, and I had no doubt that I was being deceived. The banished lover, who was following that woman only for personal gain, postponed making his peace with her for another day, and came with a gallant air to beg my beloved to make the widow's speech prophetic. Madame de Sardise remained embarrassed, having just barely recovered from the astonishment and the grief into which this conversation had plunged her. She had to endure the remarks of a man whom she did not love and who could make her look suspect to the man whom she did love. At the time I did not make such a judgment: instead, I looked upon her as a person who had deceived me, and I was very harsh when she wished to make reproaches to me. 'It is

112. Ironic reference to the heroine of Racine's tragedy of the same name (1667) who remains faithful to her dead husband, the Trojan hero Hector, despite the marriage proposal of Pyrrhus, the Greek king who holds her captive. The widow to whom she is compared thus resembles her only in the fact that she wears mourning attire. See also note 54.

fitting for you, madam,' I told her, 'to complain about something, you who are giving me so contemptible a rival. Are you not ashamed,' I continued, 'by what has just happened?' 'I admit,' she replied to me, 'that if there were the slightest foundation for your reproaches to me, I would be more at fault than you. But this man has no interest in me; I have even less interest in him, and you have seized the occasion to complain solely in order to avoid the marks of a justly founded jealousy on my part. I must spend in justifying myself a time that I had set aside for showering you with reproaches.' Then, ladies, she so clearly showed me what her conduct was that I could not refrain from begging her forgiveness. 'And you, Selincourt,' she asked me, 'how will you go about trying to appease me in this matter?' 'Ah, madam,' I replied, 'let us speak only of peace! Let there be a general amnesty, I beg you.' 'That means,' she rejoined, 'that you will pardon me for not being in the wrong, while I must pardon you for your wrongs. I consent to that,' she added, extending her hand to me; 'but no more Madame d'Ardane; for if there is a third time you will be lost.' I promised her to do that, and I kept my word. Our stroll ended with as much pleasantness as it had started with uneasiness. The widow got over her annoyance and made up with her lover the next day, as we found out. Madame de Sardise and I had a very calm love affair for a long time. More precisely, there were only the little storms necessary to re-kindle a passion; and we stopped loving each other only because everything comes to an end, and there are no eternal love affairs."

We all found Selincourt's story very pleasant. As soon as it was over, we separated, although it was still rather early, in order to go early the next morning for our last stroll in an estate that had once been magnificent, and whose remains are still very beautiful. We strolled there so long that night overtook us. There weren't any torches. The count proposed, as the best expedient, to stay at a wretched inn in the middle of the countryside, where there was barely enough food for a meal. We found it almost pleasurable to spend a night lacking comforts, since variety has so much charm. "They will be grateful to us tomorrow for our bad appearance," I whispered to Madame d'Arcire, "and those who think that this was caused by sorrow at leaving this place will not imagine that it was because of the wretched lodging." We did in fact go there, and we had a good time, because our minds were in that pleasant state where everything is conducive to joy. The sorrow of separating only surprised us as we awoke from a light slumber, which fatigue had forced upon us. We departed that very day to return to Paris. I assure you that it was with regret; for it is certain that the countryside is made for love: with fewer occupations and fewer frivolous activities than elsewhere, people love one another more tenderly.

So now I have arrived at the end of my trip. The count and the marquise are to be united forever in a few days. My parents approve of Brésy, and our marriage will take place without delay; Madame d'Orselis and the Chevalier de Chanteuil are both in search of new partners. The duke is spending his time reading Seneca, to console himself for his misfortunes in love. And as for me, madam, I wish with all my heart that I have not bored you with a rather lengthy narrative, and which was composed only of matters of small importance.

End of *A Trip to the Country*

Appendix

I have already informed the reader, at the end of my first volume, that the proverb plays that are appended to the second one are not by me. I believe that they will have more success for that reason. I have been asked to add here that the answer to each proverb will be placed only at the end of all of them, in order to leave the reader the pleasure of guessing.[113]

113. The ten proverb plays by Catherine Durand that comprise the remainder of volume 2 are not reproduced in the present edition. For an English translation of five of them, see Anne R. Larsen and Colette H. Winn, eds., *Writings by Pre-Revolutionary French Women* (New York and London: Garland, 2000), 377–402.

Selected Bibliography and Works Cited

PRINCIPAL WORKS BY THE COUNTESS DE MURAT

1697   *Mémoires de Madame la Comtesse de M****. Paris: Claude Barbin.

1698   *Contes de fées: Dédiez à Son Altesse Sérénissime Madame la Princesse Douairière de Conty; Par Mad. La Comtesse de M*****. Paris: Claude Barbin.

1698   *Les Nouveaux Contes des Fées: Par Madame de M***. Paris: Claude Barbin.

1699   *Histoires sublimes et allégoriques: Par Madame la Comtesse D**, Dédiées aux Fées Modernes*. Paris: Florentin et Pierre Delaulne.

1699   *Voyage de campagne: Par Madame la Comtesse de M****. Paris: Veuve de Claude Barbin.

April 14 1708–   *Journal pour Mademoiselle de Menou*. Paris: Bibliothèque de
June 8, 1709   l'Arsenal. Ms. no. 3471.

1710   *Les Lutins du château de Kernosy, nouvelle historique: Par Madame la Comtesse de M****. Paris: Jacques Le Febvre.

OTHER WORKS BY THE COUNTESS DE MURAT

1695   A sonnet in *Recueil de pièces curieuses et nouvelles* . . . La Haye: A. Moetjens. Vol. 3:1, 61–62.

1703   *Zatide, histoire arabe*. Paris: Pierre Ribou. [Also attributed to Eustache Le Noble.]

1714   "L'esprit folet, ou le Sylphe amoureux." In *Avantures choisies, contenant L'Amour innocent persécuté: L'esprit folet, ou le Sylphe amoureux; Le Coeur volant, ou L'Amant étourdi, Et La Belle Avanturière*. Paris: P. Prault.

1715   An Elegie, an epistle, and an eclogue in *Nouveaux choix de pièces de poésie.* La Haye: H. Van Bulderen. Vol. 1, 220–22; vol. 2, 157–61, 161–64.

1755   A chanson and an epistle in *Choix de chansons.* Paris. 45–46.

1865   A chanson and a sonnet in *Recueil de Maurepas.* Leyden. Vol. 2, 225–26; vol. 5, 56.

WORKS MISATTRIBUTED TO THE COUNTESS DE MURAT

1671   *Le Comte de Dunois.* Paris: Claude Barbin.

1695   *La Comtesse de Chateaubriand ou les Effets de la jalousie.* Paris: Théodore Guillain.

PRINCIPAL EDITIONS OF *A TRIP TO THE COUNTRY*

Murat, Henriette-Julie de Castelnau, Comtesse de. *Voyage de Campagne par Mme la Ctesse de M ***.* Paris: Veuve de Claude Barbin, 1699.

———. *Voyage de Campagne.* La Haye: Van Dols, 1700.

———. *Voyage de Campagne par Mme la Ctesse de M *** avec les Comédies en proverbes de Madame D***.* 2 vols. Paris: Prault Père, 1734.

———. "Voyage de campagne." In *Bibliothèque de campagne, ou Amusements de l'esprit et du coeur,* vol. 2. La Haye: Jean Néaulme, 1735.

———. *Les voyages de campagne.* Paris: Prault, 1737.

———. "Voyage de campagne." In *Bibliothèque de campagne, ou Amusements de l'esprit et du coeur,* vol. 2. 2nd ed. La Haye: Jean Néaulme, 1739.

———. *Voyage de campagne.* Amsterdam, 1755.

———. "Voyage de campagne." In *Voyages imaginaires, songes, visions et romans cabalistiques,* vol. 29. Amsterdam and Paris: Garnier Frères, 1788.

———. *Voyage de Campagne.* Paris: Clément Pierre Marillier, 1788.

MODERN EDITIONS OF OTHER WORKS
BY THE COUNTESS DE MURAT

"Henriette Julie de Murat." In *Beauties, Beasts and Enchantment,* edited by Jack Zipes, 129–44. London: Penguin Books, 1991.

Les fées entrent en scène. Edited by Nathalie Rizzoni. Paris: H. Champion, 2007.

"Les Nouveaux Contes des Fées." In *Nouveau Cabinet des Fées,* vol. 2, edited by

Jacques Barchilon, 201–432. Geneva: Slatkine Reprints, 1978.

Madame de Murat: Contes. Edited by Geneviève Patard. Paris: H. Champion, 2006.

"Perrault's Preface to Griselda and Murat's 'To Modern Fairies.'" Edited by Holly Tucker. *Marvels and Tales: Journal of Fairy-Tale Studies* 19, no. 1 (2005): 125–30.

"Le Prince des Feuilles." In *Le Cabinet des Fées,* edited by E. Lemirre, 555–69. Arles: Piquier, 2000.

Tra scienza e teatro: Scrittori di fiabe alla corte del Re Sole, edited by Barbara Piqué. Rome, Bulzoni, 1981.

"'Une Fée Moderne': An Unpublished Fairy Tale by la Comtesse de Murat." Edited by Ellen Welch. *Eighteenth Century Fiction* 18, no. 4 (2006): 499–510.

CRITICAL WORKS AND WORKS CITED

Argenson, René de. *Rapports inédits du lieutenant de police René d'Argenson (1697–1715) publiés d'après les manuscrits conservés à la Bibliothèque Nationale.* Edited by Paul Cottin. Paris, 1891.

Bayle, Pierre. "Jardins." In *Dictionnaire historique et critique,* Vol. 2, p. 833. Amsterdam, 1740.

Böhm, Roswitha. "La Participation des fées modernes à la création d'une mémoire féminine." *Biblio 17* 144 (2002): 119–31.

Boulay de la Merthe, Alfred. *Les Prisonniers du roi à Loches sous Louis XIV.* Tours: J. Allard, 1911.

Brocklebank, Lisa. "Rebellious Voices: The Unofficial Discourse of Cross-Dressing in d'Aulnoy, Murat and Perrault." *Children's Literature Association Quarterly* 25, no. 3 (2000): 127–36.

Cherbuliez, Juliette. *The Place of Exile: Leisure Literature and the Limits of Absolutism.* Lewisburg, PA: Bucknell University Press, 2005.

Coulet, Henri. *Le Roman jusqu'à la Révolution.* Paris: Armand Colin, 1967.

Cromer, Sylvie. *Édition du Journal pour Mademoiselle de Menou, d'après le Manuscrit 3471 de la Bibliothèque de l'Arsenal: Ouvrages de Mme la Comtesse de Murat.* Sorbonne: Thèse de 3e cycle, 1984.

———. "Le Sauvage: Histoire Sublime et allégorique de Madame de Murat." *Merveilles et contes* 1, no. 1 (1987): 2–18.

DeJean, Joan. *Tender Geographies: Women and the Origins of the Novel in France.* New York: Columbia University Press, 1991.

DiScanno, Teresa. "Les Contes de Mme de Murat ou la préciosité dans la féerie." In *Studi di Letteratura Francese: A ricordo di Franco Petralia,* 33–40. Rome: Signorelli, 1968.

Duggan, Anne. *Salonnières, Furies, and Fairies: The Politics of Gender and Cultural Change in Absolutist France.* Newark: University of Delaware Press, 2005.

———. "The Ticquet Affair as Recounted in Madame Dunoyer's *Lettres historiques et galantes:* The defiant galante femme." *Papers on French Seventeenth Century Literature* 24, no. 46 (1997): 259–76.

Engerand, Roland. *Les Rendez-vous de Loches.* Tours, 1946.

Félibien, André, sieur des Avaux et de Javercy. *Relation de la fête de Versailles du dix-huit juillet mille six cent soixante-huit: Les Divertissements de Versailles donnés par le Roi à toute sa cour au retour de la conquête de la Franche-Compté en l'année mille six cent soixante-quatorze.* Dédale: Maisonneuve et Larose, 1994.

Félix-Faure-Goyau, Lucie. *La Vie et la mort des fées, essai d'histoire littéraire.* Paris: Perrin, 1910.

Genieys-Kirk, Séverine. "Narrating the Self in Mme de Murat's Mémoires de Madame la comtesse de M*** avant sa retraite." In *Narrating the Self in Early Modern Europe,* edited by Bruno Tribout and Ruth Wheelan, 161–76. Oxford, UK: Peter Lang, 2007.

Gethner, Perry. "Playful Wit in Salon Games: The *Comedy Proverbs* of Catherine Durand." In *L'esprit en France au XVIIe siècle: Papers on French Seventeenth Century Literature,* edited by François Lagarde, 225–30. Paris: Biblio 17, 1997.

Grente, Georges, ed. *Le XVIIe siècle, Dictionnaire des Lettres françaises.* Paris: Fayard, 1996.

Guitton, Édouard. "Madame de Murat ou la fausse ingénue." *Études creusoises* 3 (1987): 203–6.

Hazard, Paul. *The European Mind: The Critical Years, 1680–1715.* Translated by J. Lewis May. Cleveland: World Publishing, 1963.

Jones Day, Shirley. *The Search for Lyonesse: Women's Fiction in France (1670–1703).* New York: Peter Lang, 1999.

Lafayette, Marie-Madeleine Pioche de la Vergne, comtesse de. *La Princesse de Clèves.* 1678. Paris: Flammarion, 1996.

Levot, Prosper. *Biographie Bretonne.* Vannes: Cauderan, 1852–57.

Lhéritier de Villandon, Marie-Jeanne. *Oeuvres meslées.* Paris: J. Guignard, 1696.

Lundlie, Marshall. "Deux précurseurs de Carmontelle: La Comtesse de Murat et Madame Durand." *Revue d'Histoire Littéraire de la France* 69 (1969):

1017–20.

Lüthi, Max. *The European Folktale: Form and Nature.* Translated by John D. Niles. Bloomington: Indiana University Press, 1982.

Marchal, Roger. *Madame de Lambert et son milieu.* Oxford, UK: Voltaire Foundation, 1991.

Michaud, Louis-Gabriel. "Murat, Henriette-Julie de Castelnau, comtesse de." In *Biographie universelle ancienne et moderne, nouvelle édition,* 29: 587. Paris: C. Delagrave, 1856.

Miorcec de Kerdanet, D.-L. *Notices chronologiques sur les théologiens, juris-consultes, philosophes, artistes, littérateurs . . . de la Bretagne.* Brest: Michel, 1818.

Nida, Eugène. *Toward a Science of Translation.* Leiden: E. J. Brill, 1964.

Nowell, Harriet. "A Ghost Story by May Mannering." *Oliver Optic's Magazine,* August 10, 1867, 399–401.

Patard, Geneviève. "Henriette-Julie de Castelnau." In *Dictionnaire des femmes de l'Ancienne France.* Paris: SIEFAR, 2007. www.siefar.org/dictionnaire/fr/ Henriette-Julie_de_Castelnau.

———. "Madame de Murat: La Vogue du conte littéraire." In *Madame de Murat: Contes,* edited by Geneviève Patard, 9–51. Paris: Champion, 2006.

———. "Madame de Murat et les fées modernes." *Romanic Review* 99, no. 3–4 (2008): 271–80.

Pilon, Edmond. *Bonnes fees d'antan.* Paris: E. Sansot, 1909.

Robert, Raymonde. *Le Conte de fées littéraire en France de la fin du XVIIe à la fin du XVIIIe siècle.* Paris: Honoré Champion, 2002.

Rivara, Annie. "Deux conceptions de la temporalité et de l'histoire, Le Voyage de Campagne de Mme de Murat (1699) et les Mémoires de d'Artagnan par Courtilz de Sandras (1700)." In *L'année 1700,* edited by Aurélia Gaillard, 91–109. Tübingen: Gunter Narr, 2004.

———. "Le Voyage de campagne comme machine à produire et à détruire des contes d'esprits." In *Le Conte merveilleux au XVIIIe siècle: Une poétique expérimentale,* edited by Régine Jomand-Baudry and Jean-François Perrin, 353–69. Paris: Kimé, 2002.

Robinson, David Michael. "The Abominable Madame de Murat." *Journal of Homosexuality* 41, no. 3–4 (2001): 53–67.

Ségalen, Auguste-Pierre. "Madame de Murat et le Limousin." In *Le Limousin au XVIIe siècle,* edited by Colloque de Limoges, 77–94. Limoges: Trames, 1979.

Seifert, Lewis. *Fairy Tales, Sexuality and Gender in France (1690–1715): Nostalgic Utopias.* Cambridge: Cambridge University Press, 1996.

————. "Pig or Prince? Murat, D'Aulnoy, and the Limits of Civilized Masculinity." In *High Anxiety: Masculinity in Crisis in Early Modern France,* edited by Kathleen P. Long, 183–209. Kirksville, MO: Truman State University Press, 2002.

Showalter, English, Jr. *The Evolution of the French Novel (1641–1782).* Princeton, NJ: Princeton University Press, 1972.

Starling, Elizabeth. "Singular Adventure of Madame Deshoulières." In *Noble Deeds of Woman; or, Examples of Female Courage and Virtue,* 317–34. Boston: Phillips, Sampson and Company, 1853.

Storer, Mary Elizabeth. *Un Épisode Littéraire de la fin du XVIIe siècle: La Mode des contes de fées (1685–1700).* Paris: Honoré Champion, 1928.

Villiers, Abbé Pierre de. *Entretiens sur les contes de fées, et sur quelques autres ouvrages du temps: Pour servir de préservatif contre le mauvais goût.* Paris: Jacques Collombat, 1699.

Welch, Marcelle Maistre. "Manipulation du discours féerique dans les Contes de fées de Mme de Murat." *Cahiers du Dix-Septième: An Interdisciplinary Journal* 5, no. 1 (1991): 21–29.

————. "Rébellion et résignation dans les contes de fées de Mme d'Aulnoy et Mme de Murat." *Cahiers du Dix-Septième: An Interdisciplinary Journal* 3, no. 2 (1989): 131–42.

Index

[*N.b.: Material indexed includes the introduction, note on the translation, and footnotes, but not the text of the novel.*]

www.ingramcontent.com/pod-product-compliance
Lightning Source LLC
Chambersburg PA
CBHW050128030726
47505CB00007B/2089